PENGUIN MODERN CLASSICS

DEATH IN VENICE
TRISTAN
TONIO KRÖGER

Thomas Mann was born in 1875 in Lübeck of a line of prosperous and influential merchants. His father was head of the ancestral firm and was twice mayor of the free city. Brought up in the company of five brothers and sisters, he completed his education under the drastic discipline of North German schoolmasters, and entered an insurance office in Munich at the age of nineteen.

Secretly he wrote his first tale, *Fallen*, and shortly afterwards left the insurance office to study art and literature at the University in Munich. After spending a year in Rome, he devoted himself exclusively to writing. His major works include *Buddenbrooks*, *Death in Venice*, *The Magic Mountain*, and the tetralogy *Joseph and his Brothers*, the first volume of which was published in 1923. He was awarded the Nobel Prize for Literature in 1929.

In 1933 Mann left Germany to live in Switzerland and then, after several previous visits, he settled in the United States, living first in Princeton, New Jersey, and later in California, where he wrote *Doctor Faustus* and *The Holy Sinner*. He revisited his native country in 1949, and in 1952 he returned to Switzerland, where *The Black Swan* and *The Confessions of Felix Krull* were written, and where he died in 1955.

THOMAS MANN

DEATH IN VENICE

TRISTAN

TONIO KRÖGER

TRANSLATED BY
H. T. LOWE-PORTER

PENGUIN BOOKS
IN ASSOCIATION WITH
SECKER & WARBURG

Penguin Books Ltd, Harmondsworth, Middlesex, England
Penguin Books Australia Ltd, Ringwood, Victoria, Australia

—

Der Tod in Venedig first published 1912
Tonio Kröger first published 1903
Tristan first published 1902
These three stories first published in English
by Secker & Warburg 1928
Published in Penguin Books 1955
Reprinted 1957, 1962, 1964, 1966, 1968, 1971, 1972, 1973

—

This translation copyright © H. T. Lowe-Porter, 1928

—

Made and printed in Great Britain
by Cox & Wyman Ltd,
London, Reading and Fakenham
Set in Monotype Bembo

CONTENTS

*

DEATH IN VENICE

*

GUSTAVE ASCHENBACH – or von Aschenbach, as he had been known officially since his fiftieth birthday – had set out alone from his house in Prince Regent Street, Munich, for an extended walk. It was a spring afternoon in that year of grace 19-, when Europe sat upon the anxious seat beneath a menace that hung over its head for months. Aschenbach had sought the open soon after tea. He was overwrought by a morning of hard, nerve-taxing work, work which had not ceased to exact his uttermost in the way of sustained concentration, conscientiousness, and tact; and after the noon meal found himself powerless to check the onward sweep of the productive mechanism within him, that *motus animi continuus* in which, according to Cicero, eloquence resides. He had sought but not found relaxation in sleep – though the wear and tear upon his system had come to make a daily nap more and more imperative – and now undertook a walk, in the hope that air and exercise might send him back refreshed to a good evening's work.

May had begun, and after weeks of cold and wet a mock summer had set in. The English Gardens, though in tenderest leaf, felt as sultry as in August and were full of vehicles and pedestrians near the city. But towards Aumeister the paths were solitary and still, and Aschenbach strolled thither, stopping awhile to watch the lively crowds in the restaurant garden with its fringe of carriages and cabs. Thence he took his homeward way outside the park and across the sunset fields. By the time he reached the North Cemetery, however, he felt tired, and a storm was brewing above Föhring; so he waited at the stopping-place for a train to carry him back to the city.

He found the neighbourhood quite empty. Not a wagon in sight, either on the paved Ungererstrasse, with its gleaming tram-lines stretching off towards Schwabing, nor on the Föhring highway. Nothing stirred behind the hedge in the stonemason's yard, where crosses, monuments, and commemorative tablets made a supernumerary and untenanted graveyard opposite the real one. The mortuary chapel, a structure in Byzantine style, stood facing it, silent in the gleam of the ebbing day. Its façade was adorned with Greek crosses and tinted hieratic designs, and displayed a symmetrically arranged selection of scriptural texts in gilded letters, all of them with a bearing upon the future life, such as: 'They are entering into the House of the Lord' and 'May the Light Everlasting shine upon them.' Aschenbach beguiled some minutes of his waiting with reading these formulas and letting his mind's eye lose itself in their mystical meaning. He was brought back to reality by the sight of a man standing in the portico, above the two apocalyptic beasts that guarded the staircase, and something not quite usual in this man's appearance gave his thoughts a fresh turn.

Whether he had come out of the hall through the bronze doors or mounted unnoticed from outside, it was impossible to tell. Aschenbach casually inclined to the first idea. He was of medium height, thin, beardless, and strikingly snub-nosed; he belonged to the red-haired type and possessed its milky, freckled skin. He was obviously not Bavarian; and the broad, straight-brimmed straw hat he had on even made him look distinctly exotic. True, he had the indigenous rucksack buckled on his back, wore a belted suit of yellowish woollen stuff, apparently frieze, and carried a grey mackintosh cape across his left forearm, which was propped against his waist. In his right hand, slantwise to the ground, he held an iron-shod stick, and braced himself against its crook, with his legs crossed. His chin was up, so that the Adam's apple looked very bald in the lean neck rising from the loose shirt: and he stood there sharply peering up into space out of colourless, red-lashed eyes, while two pronounced perpendicular furrows showed on his forehead in curious contrast to his little turned-up nose. Perhaps his heightened and heightening position helped out the impression Aschenbach received. At any rate, standing there as though at survey, the man had a bold and domineering, even a ruthless, air, and his lips completed the picture by seeming to curl back, either by reason of some deformity or else because he grimaced, being blinded by the sun in his face; they laid bare the long, white, glistening teeth to the gums.

Aschenbach's gaze, though unawares, had very likely been inquisitive and tactless; for he became suddenly conscious that the stranger was returning it, and indeed so directly, with such hostility, such plain intent to force the withdrawal of the other's eyes, that Aschenbach felt an unpleasant twinge, and turning his back, began to walk along the hedge, hastily resolving to give the man no further heed. He had forgotten him the next minute. Yet whether the pilgrim air the stranger wore kindled his fantasy or whether some other physical or psychical influence came in play, he could not tell; but he felt the most surprising consciousness of a widening of inward barriers, a kind of vaulting unrest, a youthfully ardent thirst for distant scenes – a feeling so lively and so new, or at least so long ago outgrown and forgot, that he stood there rooted to the spot, his eyes on the ground and his hands clasped behind him, exploring these sentiments of his, their bearing and scope.

True, what he felt was no more than a longing to travel; yet coming upon him with such suddenness and passion as to resemble a seizure, almost a hallucination. Desire projected itself visually: his fancy, not quite yet lulled since morning, imaged the marvels and terrors of the manifold earth. He saw. He beheld a landscape, a tropical marshland, beneath a reeking sky, steaming, monstrous, rank – a kind of primeval wilderness-world of islands, morasses, and alluvial channels. Hairy palm-trunks rose near and far out of lush brakes of fern, out of bottoms of crass vegetation, fat, swollen, thick with incredible bloom. There were trees, mis-shapen as a dream, that dropped their naked roots straight through the air into the ground or into water that was stagnant and shadowy and glassy-green, where mammoth milk-white blossoms floated, and strange high-shouldered birds with curious bills stood gazing sidewise without sound or stir. Among the knotted joints of a bamboo thicket the eyes of a crouching tiger gleamed – and he felt his heart throb with terror, yet with a longing inexplicable. Then the vision vanished. Aschenbach, shaking his head, took up his march once more along the hedge of the stonemason's yard.

He had, at least ever since he commanded means to get about the world at will, regarded travel as a necessary evil, to be endured now and again willy-nilly for the sake of one's health. Too busy with the tasks imposed upon him by his own ego and the European soul, too laden with the care and duty to create, too preoccupied to be an amateur of the gay outer world, he had been content to know as much of the earth's surface as he could without stirring far outside his own sphere – had, indeed, never even been tempted to leave Europe. Now more than ever, since his life was on the wane, since he could no longer brush aside as fanciful his artist fear of not having done, of not being finished before the works ran down, he had confined himself to close range, had hardly stepped outside the charming city which he had made his home and the rude country house he had built in the mountains, whither he went to spend the rainy summers.

And so the new impulse which thus late and suddenly swept over him was speedily made to conform to the pattern of self-discipline he had followed from his youth up. He had meant to bring his work, for which he lived, to a certain point before leaving for the country, and the thought of a leisurely ramble across the globe, which should take him away from his desk for months, was too fantastic and upsetting to be seriously entertained. Yet the source of the unexpected contagion was known to him only too well. This yearning for new and distant scenes, this craving for freedom, release, forgetfulness – they were, he admitted to himself, an impulse towards flight, flight from the spot which was the daily theatre of a rigid, cold, and passionate service. That service he loved, had even almost come to love the enervating daily struggle between a proud, tenacious, well-tried will and this growing fatigue, which no one must suspect, nor the finished product betray by any faintest sign that his inspiration could ever flag or miss fire. On the other hand, it seemed the part of common sense not to span the bow too far, not to suppress summarily a need that so unequivocally asserted itself. He thought of his work, and the place where yesterday and again to-day he had been forced to lay it down, since it would not yield either to patient effort or a swift *coup de main*. Again and again he had tried to break or untie the knot – only to retire at last from the attack with a shiver of repugnance. Yet the difficulty was actually not a great one; what sapped his strength was distaste for the task, betrayed by a fastidiousness he could no longer satisfy. In his youth, indeed, the nature and inmost essence of the literary gift had been, to him, this very scrupulosity; for it he had bridled and tempered his sensibilities, knowing full well that feeling is prone to be content with easy gains and blithe half-perfection. So now, perhaps, feeling, thus tyrannized, avenged itself by leaving him, refusing from now on to carry and wing his art and taking away with it all the ecstasy he had known in form and expression. Not that he was doing bad work. So much, at least, the years had brought him, that at any moment he might feel tranquilly assured of mastery. But he got no joy of it – not though a nation paid it homage. To him it seemed his work had ceased to be marked by that fiery play of fancy which is the product of joy, and more, and more potently, than any intrinsic content, forms in turn the joy of the receiving world. He dreaded the summer in the country, alone with the maid who prepared his food and the man who served him; dreaded to see the familiar mountain peaks and walls that would shut him up again with his heavy discontent. What he needed was a break, an interim existence, a means of passing time, other air and a new stock of blood, to make the summer tolerable and productive. Good, then, he would go a journey. Not far – not all the way to the tigers. A night in a *wagon-lit*, three or four weeks of lotus-eating at some one of the gay world's playgrounds in the lovely south. ...

So ran his thoughts, while the clang of the electric tram drew nearer down the Ungererstrasse; and as he mounted the platform he decided to devote the evening to a study of maps and railway guides. Once in, he bethought him to look back after the man in the straw hat, the companion of this brief interval which had after all been so fruitful. But he was not in his former place, nor in the tram itself, nor yet at the next stop; in short, his whereabouts remained a mystery.

Gustave Aschenbach was born at L —, a country town in the province of Silesia. He was the son of an upper official in the judicature, and his forbears had all been officers, judges, departmental functionaries – men who lived their strict, decent, sparing lives in the service of king and state. Only once before had a livelier mentality – in the quality of a clergyman – turned up among them; but swifter, more perceptive blood had in the generation before the poet's flowed into the stock from the mother's side, she being the daughter of a Bohemian musical conductor. It was from her he had the foreign traits that betrayed themselves in his appearance. The union of dry, conscientious officialdom and ardent, obscure impulse, produced an artist – and this particular artist: author of the lucid and vigorous prose epic on the life of Frederick the Great; careful, tireless weaver of the richly patterned tapestry entitled *Maia*, a novel that gathers up the threads of many human destinies in the warp of a single idea; creator of that powerful narrative *The Abject*, which taught a whole grateful generation that a man can still be capable of moral resolution even after he has plumbed the depths of knowledge; and lastly – to complete the tale of works of his mature period – the writer of that impassioned discourse on the theme of Mind and Art whose ordered force and antithetic eloquence led serious critics to rank it with Schiller's *Simple and Sentimental Poetry*.

Aschenbach's whole soul, from the very beginning, was bent on fame – and thus, while not precisely precocious, yet thanks to the unmistakable trenchancy of his personal accent he was early ripe and ready for a career. Almost before he was out of high school he had a name. Ten years later he had learned to sit at his desk and sustain and live up to his growing reputation, to write gracious and pregnant phrases in letters that must needs be brief, for many claims press upon the solid and successful man. At forty, worn down by the strains and stresses of his actual task, he had to deal with a daily post heavy with tributes from his own and foreign countries.

Remote on one hand from the banal, on the other from the eccentric, his genius was calculated to win at once the adhesion of the general public and the admiration, both sympathetic and stimulating, of the connoisseur. From childhood up he was pushed on every side to achievement, and achievement of no ordinary kind; and so his young days never knew the sweet idleness and blithe *laissez aller* that belong to youth. A nice observer once said of him in company – it was at the time when he fell ill in Vienna in his thirty-fifth year: 'You see, Aschenbach has always lived like this' – here the speaker closed the fingers of his left hand to a fist – 'never like this' – and he let his open hand hang relaxed from the back of his chair. It was apt. And this attitude was the more morally valiant in that Aschenbach was not by nature robust – he was only called to the constant tension of his career, not actually born to it.

By medical advice he had been kept from school and educated at home. He had grown up solitary, without comradeship;

yet had early been driven to see that he belonged to those whose talent is not so much out of the common as is the physical basis on which talent relies for its fulfilment. It is a seed that gives early of its fruit, whose powers seldom reach a ripe old age. But his favourite motto was 'Hold fast'; indeed, in his novel on the life of Frederick the Great he envisaged nothing else than the apotheosis of the old hero's word of command, '*Durchhalten*,' which seemed to him the epitome of fortitude under suffering. Besides, he deeply desired to live to a good old age, for it was his conviction that only the artist to whom it has been granted to be fruitful on all stages of our human scene can be truly great, or universal, or worthy of honour.

Bearing the burden of his genius, then, upon such slender shoulders and resolved to go so far, he had the more need of discipline – and discipline, fortunately, was his native inheritance from the father's side. At forty, at fifty, he was still living as he had commenced to live in the years when others are prone to waste and revel, dream high thoughts and postpone fulfilment. He began his day with a cold shower over chest and back; then, setting a pair of tall wax candles in silver holders at the head of his manuscript, he sacrificed to art, in two or three hours of almost religious fervour, the powers he had assembled in sleep. Outsiders might be pardoned for believing that his *Maia* world and the epic amplitude revealed by the life of Frederick were a manifestation of great power working under high pressure, that they came forth, as it were, all in one breath. It was the more triumph for his morale; for the truth was that they were heaped up to greatness in layer after layer, in long days of work, out of hundreds and hundreds of single inspirations; they owed their excellence, both of mass and detail, to one thing and one alone: that their creator could hold out for years under the strain of the same piece of work, with an endurance and a tenacity of purpose like that which had conquered his native province of Silesia, <u>devoting to actual</u> <u>composition none but his best and freshest hours.</u>

For an intellectual product of any value to exert an immediate influence which shall also be deep and lasting, it must rest on an inner harmony, yes, an affinity, between the personal destiny of its author and that of his contemporaries in general. Men do not know why they award fame to one work of art rather than another. Without being in the faintest connoisseurs, they think to justify the warmth of their commendations by discovering in it a hundred virtues, whereas the real ground of their applause is inexplicable – it is sympathy. Aschenbach had once given direct expression – though in an unobtrusive place – to the idea that almost everything conspicuously great is great in despite: has come into being in defiance of affliction and pain, poverty, destitution, bodily weakness, vice, passion, and a thousand other obstructions. And that was more than observation – it was the fruit of experience, it was precisely the formula of his life and fame, it was the key to his work. What wonder, then, if it was also the fixed character, the outward gesture, of his most individual figures?

The new type of hero favoured by Aschenbach, and recurring many times in his works, had early been analysed by a shrewd critic: 'The conception of an intellectual and virginal manliness, which clenches its teeth and stands in modest defiance of the swords and spears that pierce its side.' That was beautiful, it was *spirituel*, it was exact, despite the suggestion of too great passivity it held. Forbearance in the face of fate, beauty constant under torture, are not merely passive. They are a positive achievement, an explicit triumph; and the figure of Sebastian is the most beautiful symbol, if not of art as a whole, yet certainly of the art we speak of here. Within that world of Aschenbach's creation were exhibited many phases of this theme: there was the aristocratic self-command that is eaten out within and for as long as it can conceals its biologic decline from the eyes of the world; the sere and ugly outside, hiding the embers of smouldering fire – and having power to fan them to so pure a flame as to challenge supremacy in the domain of beauty itself; the pallid languors of the flesh, contrasted with the fiery ardours of the spirit within, which can fling a whole proud people down at the foot of the Cross, at the feet of its own sheer self-abnegation; the gracious bearing preserved in the stern, stark service of form; the unreal, precarious existence of the born intrigant with its swiftly enervating alternation of schemes and desires – all these human fates and many more of their like one read in Aschenbach's pages, and reading them might doubt the existence of any other kind of heroism than the heroism born of weakness. And, after all, what kind could be truer to the spirit of the times? Gustave Aschenbach was the poet-spokesman of all those who labour at the edge of exhaustion; of the overburdened, of those who are already worn out but still hold themselves upright; of all our modern moralizers of accomplishment, with stunted growth and scanty resources, who yet contrive by skilful husbanding and prodigious spasms of will to produce, at least for a while, the effect of greatness. There are many such, they are the heroes of the age. And in Aschenbach's pages they saw themselves; he justified, he exalted them, he sang their praise – and they, they were grateful, they heralded his fame.

He had been young and crude with the times and by them badly counselled. He had taken false steps, blundered, exposed himself, offended in speech and writing against tact and good sense. But he had attained to honour, and honour, he used to say, is the natural goal towards which every considerable talent presses with whip and spur. Yes, one might put it that his whole career had been one conscious and overweening ascent to honour, which left in the rear all the misgivings or self-derogation which might have hampered him.

What pleases the public is lively and vivid delineation which makes no demands on the intellect; but passionate and absolutist youth can only be enthralled by a problem. And Aschenbach was as absolute, as problematist, as any youth of them all. He had done homage to intellect, had overworked the soil of knowledge and ground up her seed-corn; had turned his back on the 'mysteries', called genius itself in question, held up art to scorn – yes, even while his faithful following revelled in the characters he created, he, the young artist, was taking away the breath of the twenty-year-olds with his cynic utterances on the nature of art and the artist life.

But it seems that a noble and active mind blunts itself against nothing so quickly as the sharp and bitter irritant of knowledge. And certain it is that the youth's constancy of purpose, no matter how painfully conscientious, was shallow beside the mature resolution of the master of his craft, who made a right-about-face, turned his back on the realm of knowledge, and passed it by with averted face, lest it lame his will or power of action, paralyse his feelings or his passions, deprive any of these of their conviction or utility. How else interpret the oft-cited story of *The Abject* than as a rebuke to the excesses of a psychology-ridden age, embodied in the delineation of the weak and silly fool who manages to lead fate by the nose; driving his wife, out of sheer innate pusillanimity, into the arms of a beardless youth, and making this disaster an excuse for trifling away the rest of his life?

With rage the author here rejects the rejected, casts out the outcast – and the measure of his fury is the measure of his condemnation of all moral shilly-shallying. Explicitly he renounces sympathy with the abyss, explicitly he refutes the flabby humanitarianism of the phrase: '*Tout comprendre c'est tout pardonner.*' What was here unfolding, or rather was already in full bloom, was the 'miracle of regained detachment', which a little later became the theme of one of the author's dialogues, dwelt upon not without a certain oracular emphasis. Strange sequence of thought! Was it perhaps an intellectual consequence of this rebirth, this new austerity, that from now on his style showed an almost exaggerated sense of beauty, a lofty purity, symmetry, and simplicity, which gave his productions a stamp of the classic, of conscious and deliberate mastery? And yet: this moral fibre, surviving the hampering and disintegrating effect of knowledge, does it not result in its turn in a dangerous simplification, in a tendency to equate the world and the human soul, and thus to strengthen the hold of the evil, the forbidden, and the ethically impossible? And has not form two aspects? Is it not moral and immoral at once; moral in so far as it is the expression and result of discipline, immoral – yes, actually hostile to morality – in that of its very essence it is indifferent to good and evil, and deliberately concerned to make the moral world stoop beneath its proud and undivided sceptre?

Be that as it may. Development is destiny; and why should a career attended by applause and adulation of the masses necessarily take the same course as one which does not share the glamour and the obligations of fame? Only the incorrigible bohemian smiles or scoffs when a man of transcendent gifts outgrows his carefree prentice stage, recognizes his own worth and forces the world to recognize it too and pay it homage, though he puts on a courtly bearing to hide his bitter struggles and his loneliness. Again, the play of a developing talent must give its possessor joy, if of a wilful, defiant kind. With time, an official note, something almost expository, crept into Gustave Aschenbach's method. His later style gave up the old sheer audacities, the fresh and subtle nuances – it became fixed and exemplary, conservative, formal, even formulated. Like Louis XIV – or as tradition has it of him – Aschenbach, as he went on in years, banished from his style every common word. It was at this time that the school authorities adopted selections from his works into their text-books. And he found it only fitting – and had not thought but to accept – when a German prince signalized his accession to the throne by conferring upon the poet-author of the life of Frederick the Great on his fiftieth birthday the letters-patent of nobility.

He had roved about for a few years, trying this place and

that as a place of residence, before choosing, as he soon did, the city of Munich for his permanent home. And there he lived, enjoying among his fellow-citizens the honour which is in rare cases the reward of intellectual eminence. He married young, the daughter of a university family; but after a brief term of wedded happiness his wife had died. A daughter, already married, remained to him. A son he never had.

Gustave von Aschenbach was somewhat below middle height, dark and smooth-shaven, with a head that looked rather too large for his almost delicate figure. He wore his hair brushed back; it was thin at the parting, bushy and grey on the temples, framing a lofty, rugged, knotty brow – if one may so characterize it. The nose-piece of his rimless gold spectacles cut into the base of his thick, aristocratically hooked nose. The mouth was large, often lax, often suddenly narrow and tense; the cheeks lean and furrowed, the pronounced chin slightly cleft. The vicissitudes of fate, it seemed, must have passed over his head, for he held it, plaintively, rather on one side; yet it was art, not the stern discipline of an active career, that had taken over the office of modelling these features. Behind this brow were born the flashing thrust and parry of the dialogue between Frederick and Voltaire on the theme of war; these eyes, weary and sunken, gazing through their glasses, had beheld the blood-stained inferno of the hospitals in the Seven Years' War. Yes, personally speaking too, art heightens life. She gives deeper joy, she consumes more swiftly. She engraves adventures of the spirit and the mind in the faces of her votaries; let them lead outwardly a life of the most cloistered calm, she will in the end produce in them a fastidiousness, an over-refinement, a nervous fever and exhaustion, such as a career of extravagant passions and pleasures can hardly show.

Eager though he was to be off, Aschenbach was kept in Munich by affairs both literary and practical for some two weeks after that walk of his. But at length he ordered his country home put ready against his return within the next few weeks, and on a day between the middle and the end of May took the evening train for Trieste, where he stopped only twenty-four hours, embarking for Pola the next morning but one.

What he sought was a fresh scene, without associations, which should yet be not too out-of-the-way; and accordingly he chose an island in the Adriatic, not far off the Istrian coast. It had been well known some years, for its splendidly rugged cliff formations on the side next the open sea, and its population, clad in a bright flutter of rags and speaking an outlandish tongue. But there was rain and heavy air; the society at the hotel was provincial Austrian, and limited; besides, it annoyed him not to be able to get at the sea – he missed the close and soothing contact which only a gentle sandy slope affords. He could not feel this was the place he sought; an inner impulse made him wretched, urging him on he knew not whither; he racked his brains, he looked up boats, then all at once his goal stood plain before his eyes. But of course! When one wanted to arrive overnight at the incomparable, the fabulous, the like-nothing-else-in-the-world, where was it one went? Why, obviously; he had intended to go there, what ever was he doing here? A blunder. He made all haste to correct it, announcing his departure at once. Ten days after his arrival on the island a swift motor-boat bore him and his luggage in the misty dawning back across the water to the naval station, where he landed only to pass over the landing-stage and on to the wet decks of a ship lying there with steam up for the passage to Venice.

It was an ancient hulk belonging to an Italian line, obsolete, dingy, grimed with soot. A dirty hunchbacked sailor, smirkingly polite, conducted him at once belowships to a cavernous, lamplit cabin. There behind a table sat a man with a beard like a goat's; he had his hat on the back of his head, a cigarstump in the corner of his mouth; he reminded Aschenbach of an old-fashioned circus-director. This person put the usual questions and wrote out a ticket to Venice, which he issued to the traveller with many commercial flourishes.

'A ticket for Venice,' he repeated, stretching out his arm to dip the pen into the thick ink in a tilted ink-stand. 'One first-class to Venice! Here you are, *signore mio*.' He made some scrawls on the paper, strewed bluish sand on it out of a box, thereafter letting the sand run off into an earthen vessel, folded the paper with bony yellow fingers, and wrote on the outside. 'An excellent choice,' he rattled on. 'Ah, Venice! What a glorious city! Irresistibly attractive to the cultured man for her past history as well as her present charm.' His copious gesturings and empty phrases gave the odd impression that he feared the traveller might alter his mind. He changed Aschenbach's note, laying the money on the spotted table-cover with the glibness of a croupier. 'A pleasant visit to you, signore,' he said, with a melodramatic bow. 'Delighted to serve you.' Then he beckoned and called out: 'Next' as though a stream of passengers stood waiting to be served, though in point of fact there was not one. Aschenbach returned to the upper deck.

He leaned an arm on the railing and looked at the idlers lounging along the quay to watch the boat go out. Then he turned his attention to his fellow-passengers. Those of the second class, both men and women, were squatted on their bundles of luggage on the forward deck. The first cabin consisted of a group of lively youths, clerks from Pola, evidently, who had made up a pleasure excursion to Italy and were not a little thrilled at the prospect, bustling about and laughing with satisfaction at the stir they made. They leaned over the railings and shouted, with a glib command of epithet, derisory remarks at such of their fellow-clerks as they saw going to business along the quay; and these in turn shook their sticks and shouted as good back again. One of the party, in a dandi-fied buff suit, a rakish panama with a coloured scarf, and a red cravat, was loudest of the loud: he outcrowed all the rest. Aschenbach's eye dwelt on him, and he was shocked to see that the apparent youth was no youth at all. He was an old man, beyond a doubt, with wrinkles and crow's-feet round eyes and mouth; the dull carmine of the cheeks was rouge, the brown hair a wig. His neck was shrunken and sinewy, his turned-up moustaches and small imperial were dyed, and the unbroken double row of yellow teeth he showed when he laughed were but too obviously a cheapish false set. He wore a seal ring on each forefinger, but the hands were those of an old man. Aschenbach was moved to shudder as he watched the creature and his association with the rest of the group. Could they not see he was old, that he had no right to wear the clothes they wore or pretend to be one of them? But they were used to him, it seemed; they suffered him among them, they paid back his jokes in kind and the playful pokes in the ribs he gave them. How could they? Aschenbach put his hand to his brow, he covered his eyes, for he had slept little, and they smarted. He felt not quite canny, as though the world were suffering a dreamlike distortion of perspective which he might arrest by shutting it all out for a few minutes and then looking at it afresh. But instead he felt a floating sensation, and opened his eyes with unreasoning alarm to find that the ship's dark sluggish bulk was slowly leaving the jetty. Inch by inch, with the to-and-fro motion of her machinery, the strip of iridescent dirty water widened, the boat manoeuvred clumsily and turned her bow to the open sea. Aschenbach moved over to the starboard side, where the hunchbacked sailor had set up a deck-chair for him, and a steward in a greasy dress-coat asked for orders.

The sky was grey, the wind humid. Harbour and island dropped behind, all sight of land soon vanished in mist. Flakes of sodden, clammy soot fell upon the still undried deck. Before the boat was an hour out a canvas had to be spread as a shelter from the rain.

Wrapped in his cloak, a book in his lap, our traveller rested; the hours slipped by unawares. It stopped raining, the canvas was taken down. The horizon was visible right round: beneath the sombre dome of the sky stretched the vast plain of empty sea. But immeasurable unarticulated space weakens our power to measure time as well: the time-sense falters and grows dim. Strange, shadowy figures passed and repassed – the elderly coxcomb, the goat-bearded man from the bowels of the ship – with vague gesturings and mutterings through the traveller's mind as he lay. He fell asleep.

At midday he was summoned to luncheon in a corridor-like saloon with the sleeping-cabins giving off it. He ate at the head of the long table; the party of clerks, including the old man, sat with the jolly captain at the other end, where they had been carousing since ten o'clock. The meal was wretched, and soon done. Aschenbach was driven to seek the open and look at the sky – perhaps it would lighten presently above Venice.

He had not dreamed it could be otherwise, for the city had ever given him a brilliant welcome. But sky and sea remained leaden, with spurts of fine, mistlike rain; he reconciled himself to the idea of seeing a different Venice from that he had always approached on the landward side. He stood by the foremast, his gaze on the distance, alert for the first glimpse of the coast. And he thought of the melancholy and susceptible poet who had once seen the towers and turrets of his dreams rise out of these waves; repeated the rhythms born of his awe, his mingled emotions of joy and suffering – and easily susceptible to a prescience already shaped with him, he asked his own sober, weary heart if a new enthusiasm, a new preoccupation, some late adventure of the feelings could still be in store for the idle traveller.

The flat coast showed on the right, the sea was soon populous with fishing-boats. The Lido appeared and was left behind as the ship glided at half speed through the narrow harbour of the same name, coming to a full stop on the lagoon in sight of garish, badly built houses. Here it waited for the boat bringing the sanitary inspector.

An hour passed. One had arrived – and yet not. There was no conceivable haste – yet one felt harried. The youths from Pola were on deck, drawn hither by the martial sound of horns coming across the water from the direction of the Public Gardens. They had drunk a good deal of Asti and were moved to shout and hurrah at the drilling *bersaglieri*. But the young-old man was a truly repulsive sight in the condition to which his company with youth had brought him. He could not carry his wine like them: he was pitiably drunk. He swayed as he stood – watery-eyed, a cigarette between his shaking fingers, keeping upright with difficulty. He could not have taken a step without falling and knew better than to stir, but his spirits were deplorably high. He buttonholed anyone who came within reach, he stuttered, he giggled, he leered, he fatuously shook his beringed old forefinger; his tongue kept seeking the corner of his mouth in a suggestive motion ugly to behold. Aschenbach's brow darkened as he looked, and there came over him once more a dazed sense, as though things about him were just slightly losing their ordinary perspective, beginning to show a distortion that might merge into the grotesque. He was prevented from dwelling on the feeling, for now the machinery began to thud again, and the ship took up its passage through the Canal di San Marco which had been interrupted so near the goal.

He saw it once more, that landing-place that takes the breath away, that amazing group of incredible structures the Republic set up to meet the awe-struck eye of the approaching seafarer: the airy splendour of the palace and Bridge of Sighs, the columns of lion and saint on the shore, the glory of the projecting flank of the fairy temple, the vista of gateway and clock. Looking, he thought that to come to Venice by the station is like entering a palace by the back door. No one should approach, save by the high seas as he was doing now, this most improbable of cities.

The engines stopped. Gondolas pressed alongside, the landing-stairs were let down, customs officials came on board and did their office, people began to go ashore. Aschenbach ordered a gondola. He meant to take up his abode by the sea and needed to be conveyed with his luggage to the landing-stage of the little steamers that ply between the city and the Lido. They called down his order to the surface of the water where the gondoliers were quarrelling in dialect. Then came another delay while his trunk was worried down the ladder-like stairs. Thus he was forced to endure the importunities of the ghastly young-old man, whose drunken state obscurely urged him to pay the stranger the honour of a formal farewell. 'We wish you a very pleasant sojourn,' he babbled, bowing and scraping. 'Pray keep us in mind. *Au revoir, excusez et bon jour, votre Excellence.*' He drooled, he blinked, he licked the corner of his mouth, the little imperial bristled on his elderly chin. He put the tips of two fingers to his mouth and said thickly: 'Give her our love, will you, the p-pretty little dear' – here his upper plate came away and fell down on the lower one. . . . Aschenbach escaped. 'Little sweety-sweety-sweetheart' he heard behind him, gurgled and stuttered, as he climbed down the rope stair into the boat.

Is there anyone but must repress a secret thrill, on arriving in Venice for the first time – or returning thither after long absence – and stepping into a Venetian gondola? That singular conveyance, come down unchanged from ballad times, black as nothing else on earth except a coffin – what pictures it calls up of lawless, silent adventures in the plashing night; or even more, what visions of death itself, the bier and solemn rites and last soundless voyage! And has anyone remarked that the seat in such a bark, the arm-chair lacquered in coffin-black, and dully black-upholstered, is the softest, most luxurious, most relaxing seat in the world? Aschenbach realized it when he had let himself down at the gondolier's feet, opposite his luggage, which lay neatly composed on the vessel's beak. The rowers still gestured fiercely; he heard their harsh, incoherent tones. But the strange stillness of the water-city seemed to take up their voices gently, to disembody and scatter them over the sea. It was warm here in the harbour. The lukewarm air of the sirocco breathed upon him, he leaned back among his cushions and gave himself to the yielding element, closing his eyes for very pleasure in an indolence as unaccustomed as sweet. 'The trip will be short,' he thought, and wished it might last forever. They gently swayed away from the boat with its bustle and clamour of voices.

It grew still and stiller all about. No sound but the splash of the oars, the hollow slap of the wave against the steep, black, halbert-shaped beak of the vessel, and one sound more – a muttering by fits and starts, expressed as it were by the motion of his arms, from the lips of the gondolier. He was talking to himself, between his teeth. Aschenbach glanced up and saw with surprise that the lagoon was widening, his vessel was headed for the open sea. Evidently it would not do to give himself up to sweet *far niente*; he must see his wishes carried out.

'You are to take me to the steamboat landing, you know,' he said, half turning round towards it. The muttering stopped. There was no reply.

'Take me to the steamboat landing,' he repeated, and this time turned quite round and looked up into the face of the gondolier as he stood there on his little elevated deck, high against the pale grey sky. The man had an unpleasing, even brutish face, and wore blue clothes like a sailor's, with a yellow sash; a shapeless straw hat with the braid torn at the brim perched rakishly on his head. His facial structure, as well as the curling blond moustache under the short snub nose, showed him to be of non-Italian stock. Physically rather undersized, so that one would not have expected him to be very muscular, he pulled vigorously at the oar, putting all his body-weight behind each stroke. Now and then the effort he made curled back his lips and bared his white teeth to the gums. He spoke in a decided, almost curt voice, looking out to sea over his fare's head: 'The signore is going to the Lido.'

Aschenbach answered: 'Yes, I am. But I only took the gondola to cross over to San Marco. I am using the *vaporetto* from there.'

'But the signore cannot use the *vaporetto*.'

'And why not?'

'Because the *vaporetto* does not take luggage.'

It was true. Aschenbach remembered it. He made no answer. But the man's gruff, overbearing manner, so unlike the usual courtesy of his countrymen towards the stranger, was intolerable. Aschenbach spoke again: 'That is my own affair. I may want to give my luggage in deposit. You will turn round.'

No answer. The oar splashed, the wave struck dull against the prow. And the muttering began anew, the gondolier talked to himself, between his teeth.

What should the traveller do? Alone on the water with this tongue-tied, obstinate, uncanny man, he saw no way of enforcing his will. And if only he did not excite himself, how pleasantly he might rest! Had he not wished the voyage might last forever? The wisest thing – and how much the pleasantest! – was to let matters take their own course. A spell of indolence was upon him; it came from the chair he sat in – this low, black-upholstered arm-chair, so gently rocked at the hands of the despotic boatman in his rear. The thought passed dreamily through Aschenbach's brain that perhaps he had fallen into the clutches of a criminal; it had not power to rouse him to action. More annoying was the simpler explanation: that the man was only trying to extort money. A sense of duty, a recollection, as it were, that this ought to be prevented, made him collect himself to say:

'How much do you ask for the trip?'

And the gondolier, gazing out over his head, replied: 'The signore will pay.'

There was an established reply to this; Aschenbach made it, mechanically:

'I will pay nothing whatever if you do not take me where I want to go.'

'The signore wants to go to the Lido.'

'But not with you.'

'I am a good rower, signore, I will row you well.'

'So much is true,' thought Aschenbach, and again he relaxed. 'That is true, you row me well. Even if you mean to rob me, even if you hit me in the back with your oar and send me down to the kingdom of Hades, even then you will have rowed me well.'

But nothing of the sort happened. Instead, they fell in with company: a boat came alongside and waylaid them, full of men and women singing to guitar and mandolin. They rowed persistently bow for bow with the gondola and filled the silence that had rested on the waters with their lyric love of gain. Aschenbach tossed money into the hat they held out. The music stopped at once, they rowed away. And once more the gondolier's mutter became audible as he talked to himself in fits and snatches.

Thus they rowed on, rocked by the wash of a steamer returning citywards. At the landing two municipal officials were walking up and down with their hands behind their backs and their faces turned towards the lagoon. Aschenbach was helped on shore by the old man with a boat-hook who is the permanent feature of every landing-stage in Venice; and having no small change to pay the boatman, crossed over into the hotel opposite. His wants were supplied in the lobby, but when he came back his possessions were already on a hand-car on the quay, and gondola and gondolier were gone.

'He ran away, signore,' said the old boatman. 'A bad lot, a man without a licence. He is the only gondolier without one. The others telephoned over, and he knew we were on the look-out, so he made off.'

Aschenbach shrugged.

'The signore has had a ride for nothing,' said the old man, and held out his hat. Aschenbach dropped some coins. He directed that his luggage be taken to the Hôtel des Bains and followed the hand-car through the avenue, that white-blossoming avenue with taverns, booths, and pensions on either side it, which runs across the island diagonally to the beach.

He entered the hotel from the garden terrace at the back and passed through the vestibule and hall into the office. His arrival was expected, and he was served with courtesy and dispatch. The manager, a small, soft, dapper man with a black moustache and a caressing way with him, wearing a French frock-coat, himself took him up in the lift and showed him his room. It was a pleasant chamber, furnished in cherry-wood, with lofty windows looking out to sea. It was decorated with strong-scented flowers. Aschenbach, as soon as he was alone, and while they brought in his trunk and bags and disposed them in the room, went up to one of the windows and stood looking out upon the beach in its afternoon emptiness, and at the sunless sea, now full and sending long, low waves with rhythmic beat upon the sand.

A solitary, unused to speaking of what he sees and feels, has mental experiences which are at once more intense and less articulate than those of a gregarious man. They are sluggish, yet more wayward, and never without a melancholy tinge. Sights and impressions which others brush aside with a glance, a light comment, a smile, occupy him more than their due; they sink silently in, they take on meaning, they become experience, emotion, adventure. Solitude gives birth to the original in us, to beauty unfamiliar and perilous – to poetry. But also, it gives birth to the opposite: to the perverse, the illicit, the absurd. Thus the traveller's mind still dwelt with disquiet on the episodes of his journey hither: on the horrible old fop with his drivel about a mistress, on the outlaw boatman and his lost tip. They did not offend his reason, they hardly afforded food for thought; yet they seemed by their very nature fundamentally strange, and thereby vaguely disquieting. Yet here was the sea; even in the midst of such thoughts he saluted it with his eyes, exulting that Venice was near and accessible. At length he turned round, disposed his personal belongings and made certain arrangements with the chambermaid for his comfort, washed, and was conveyed to the ground floor by the green-uniformed Swiss who ran the lift.

He took tea on the terrace facing the sea and afterwards went down and walked some distance along the shore promenade in the direction of Hôtel Excelsior. When he came back it seemed to be time to change for dinner. He did so, slowly and methodically as his way was, for he was accustomed to work while he dressed; but even so he found himself a little early when he entered the hall, where a large number of guests had collected – strangers to each other and affecting mutual indifference, yet united in expectancy of the meal. He picked up a paper, sat down in a leather arm-chair, and took stock of the company, which compared most favourably with that he had just left.

This was a broad and tolerant atmosphere, of wide horizons. Subdued voices were speaking most of the principal European tongues. That uniform of civilization, the conventional evening dress, gave outward conformity to the varied types. There were long, dry Americans, large-familied Russians, English ladies, German children with French *bonnes*. The Slavic element predominated, it seemed. In Aschenbach's neighbourhood Polish was being spoken.

Round a wicker table next him was gathered a group of young folk in charge of a governess or companion – three young girls, perhaps fifteen to seventeen years old, and a long-haired boy of about fourteen. Aschenbach noticed with astonishment the lad's perfect beauty. His face recalled the noblest moment of Greek sculpture – pale, with a sweet reserve, with clustering honey-coloured ringlets, the brow and nose descending in one line, the winning mouth, the expression of pure and godlike serenity. Yet with all this chaste perfection of form it was of such unique personal charm that the observer thought he had never seen, either in nature or art, anything so utterly happy and consummate. What struck him further was the strange contrast the group afforded, a difference in educational method, so to speak, shown in the way the brother and sisters were clothed and treated. The girls, the eldest of whom was practically grown up, were dressed with an almost disfiguring austerity. All three wore half-length slate-coloured frocks of cloister-like plainness, arbitrarily unbecoming in cut, with white turn-over collars as their only adornment. Every grace of outline was wilfully suppressed; their hair lay smoothly plastered to their heads, giving them a vacant expression, like a nun's. All this could only be by the mother's orders; but there was no trace of the same pedagogic severity in the case of the boy. Tenderness and softness, it was plain, conditioned his existence. No scissors had been put to the lovely hair that (like the Spinnario's) curled about his brows, above his ears, longer still in the neck. He wore an English sailor suit, with quilted sleeves that narrowed round the delicate wrists of his long and slender though still childish hands. And this suit, with its breast-knot, lacings, and embroideries, lent the slight figure something 'rich and strange', a spoilt, exquisite air. The observer saw him in half profile, with one foot in its black patent leather advanced, one elbow resting on the arm of his basket-chair, the cheek nestled into the closed hand in a pose of easy grace, quite unlike the stiff subservient mien which was evidently habitual to his sisters. Was he delicate? His facial tint was ivory-white against the golden darkness of his clustering locks. Or was he simply a pampered darling, the object of a self-willed and partial love? Aschenbach inclined to think the latter. For in almost every artist nature is inborn a wanton and treacherous proneness to side with the beauty that breaks hearts, to single out aristocratic pretensions and pay them homage.

A waiter announced, in English, that dinner was served. Gradually the company dispersed through the glass doors into the dining-room. Late-comers entered from the vestibule or the lifts. Inside, dinner was being served; but the young Poles still sat and waited about their wicker table. Aschenbach felt comfortable in his deep arm-chair, he enjoyed the beauty before his eyes, he waited with them.

The governess, a short, stout, red-faced person, at length gave the signal. With lifted brows she pushed back her chair and made a bow to the tall woman, dressed in palest grey, who now entered the hall. This lady's abundant jewels were pearls, her manner was cool and measured; the fashion of her gown and the arrangement of her lightly powdered hair had the simplicity prescribed in certain circles whose piety and aristocracy are equally marked. She might have been, in Germany, the wife of some high official. But there was something faintly fabulous, after all, in her appearance, though lent it solely by the pearls she wore: they were well-nigh priceless, and consisted of ear-rings and a three-stranded necklace, very long, with gems the size of cherries.

The brother and sisters had risen briskly. They bowed over their mother's hand to kiss it, she turning away from them, with a slight smile on her face, which was carefully preserved but rather sharp-nosed and worn. She addressed a few words in French to the governess, then moved towards the glass door. The children followed, the girls in order of age, then the governess, and last the boy. He chanced to turn before he crossed the threshold, and as there was no one else in the room, his strange, twilit grey eyes met Aschenbach's, as our traveller sat there with the paper on his knee, absorbed in looking after the group.

There was nothing singular, of course, in what he had seen. They had not gone in to dinner before their mother, they had waited, given her a respectful salute, and but observed the right and proper forms on entering the room. Yet they had done all this so expressly, with such self-respecting dignity, discipline, and sense of duty that Aschenbach was impressed. He lingered still a few minutes, then he, too, went into the dining-room, where he was shown to a table far off from the Polish family, as he noted at once, with a stirring of regret.

Tired, yet mentally alert, he beguiled the long, tedious meal with abstract, even with transcendent matters: pondered the mysterious harmony that must come to subsist between the individual human being and the universal law, in order that human beauty may result; passed on to general problems of form and art, and came at length to the conclusion that what seemed to him fresh and happy thoughts were like the flattering inventions of a dream, which the waking sense proves worthless and insubstantial. He spent the evening in the park, that was sweet with the odours of evening – sitting, smoking, wandering about; went to bed betimes, and passed the night in deep, unbroken sleep, visited, however, by varied and lively dreams.

The weather next day was no more promising. A land breeze blew. Beneath a colourless, overcast sky the sea lay sluggish, and as it were shrunken, so far withdrawn as to leave bare several rows of long sand-banks. The horizon looked close and prosaic. When Aschenbach opened his window he thought he smelt the stagnant odour of the lagoons.

He felt suddenly out of sorts and already began to think of leaving. Once, years before, after weeks of bright spring weather, this wind had found him out; it had been so bad as to force him to flee from the city like a fugitive. And now it seemed beginning again – the same feverish distaste, the pressure on his temples, the heavy eyelids. It would be a nuisance to change again; but if the wind did not turn, this was no place for him. To be on the safe side, he did not entirely unpack. At nine o'clock he went down to the buffet, which lay between the hall and the dining-room and served as breakfast-room.

A solemn stillness reigned here, such as it is the ambition of all large hotels to achieve. The waiters moved on noiseless feet. A rattling of tea-things, a whispered word – and no other sounds. In a corner diagonally to the door, two tables off his own, Aschenbach saw the Polish girls with their governess. They sat there very straight, in their stiff blue linen frocks with little turn-over collars and cuffs, their ash-blond hair newly brushed flat, their eyelids red from sleep, and handed each other the marmalade. They had nearly finished their meal. The boy was not there.

Aschenbach smiled. 'Aha, little Phaeax,' he thought. 'It seems you are privileged to sleep yourself out.' With sudden gaiety he quoted:

'*Oft veränderten Schmuck und warme Bäder und Ruhe.*'

He took a leisurely breakfast. The porter came up with his braided cap in his hand, to deliver some letters that had been sent on. Aschenbach lighted a cigarette and opened a few letters and thus was still seated to witness the arrival of the sluggard.

He entered through the glass doors and walked diagonally across the room to his sisters at their table. He walked with extraordinary grace – the carriage of the body, the action of the knee, the way he set down his foot in its white shoe – it was all so light, it was at once dainty and proud, it wore an added charm in the childish shyness which made him twice turn his head as he crossed the room, made him give a quick glance and then drop his eyes. He took his seat, with a smile and a murmured word in his soft and blurry tongue; and Aschenbach, sitting so that he could see him in profile, was astonished anew, yes, startled, at the godlike beauty of the human being. The lad had on a light sailor suit of blue and white striped cotton, with a red silk breast-knot and a simple white standing collar round the neck – a not very elegant effect – yet above this collar the head was poised like a flower, in incomparable loveliness. It was the head of Eros, with the yellowish bloom of Parian marble, with fine serious brows, and dusky clustering ringlets standing out in soft plenteousness over temples and ears.

'Good, oh, very good indeed!' thought Aschenbach, assuming the patronizing air of the connoisseur to hide, as artists will, their ravishment over a masterpiece. 'Yes,' he went on to himself, 'if it were not that sea and beach were waiting for me, I should sit here as long as you do.' But he went out on that, passing through the hall, beneath the watchful eye of the functionaries, down the steps and directly across the board walk to the section of the beach reserved for the guests of the hotel. The bathing-master, a barefoot old man in linen trousers and sailor blouse, with a straw hat, showed him the cabin that had been rented for him, and Aschenbach had him set up table and chair on the sandy platform before it. Then he dragged the reclining-chair through the pale yellow sand, closer to the sea, sat down, and composed himself.

He delighted, as always, in the scene on the beach, the sight of sophisticated society giving itself over to a simple life at the edge of the element. The shallow grey sea was already gay with children wading, with swimmers, with figures in bright colours lying on the sand-banks with arms behind their heads. Some were rowing in little keelless boats painted red and blue, and laughing when they capsized. A long row of *capanne* ran down the beach, with platforms, where people sat as on verandas, and there was social life, with bustle and with indolent repose; visits were paid, amid much chatter, punctilious morning toilettes hob-nobbed with comfortable and privileged dishabille. On the hard wet sand close to the sea figures in white bath-robes or loose wrappings in garish colours strolled up and down. A mammoth sand-hill had been built up on Aschenbach's right, the work of children, who had stuck it full of tiny flags. Vendors of sea-shells, fruit, and cakes knelt beside their wares spread out on the sand. A row of cabins on

the left stood obliquely to the others and to the sea, thus forming the boundary of the enclosure on this side; and on the
little veranda in front of one of these a Russian family was
encamped; bearded men with strong white teeth, ripe, indolent women, a Fräulein from the Baltic provinces, who sat at
an easel painting the sea and tearing her hair in despair; two
ugly but good-natured children and an old maidservant in a
head-cloth, with the caressing, servile manner of the born
dependent. There they sat together in grateful enjoyment of
their blessings: constantly shouting at their romping children,
who paid not the slightest heed; making jokes in broken
Italian to the funny old man who sold them sweetmeats, kissing each other on the cheeks – no jot concerned that their
domesticity was overlooked.

'I'll stop,' thought Aschenbach. 'Where could it be better
than here?' With his hands clasped in his lap he let his eyes
swim in the wideness of the sea, his gaze lose focus, blur, and
grow vague in the misty immensity of space. His love of the
ocean had profound sources: the hard-worked artist's longing
for rest, his yearning to seek refuge from the thronging manifold shapes of his fancy in the bosom of the simple and vast;
and another yearning, opposed to his art and perhaps for that
very reason a lure, for the unorganized, the immeasurable,
the eternal – in short, for nothingness. He whose preoccupation is with excellence longs fervently to find rest in perfection; and is not nothingness a form of perfection? As he sat
there dreaming thus, deep, deep into the void, suddenly the
margin line of the shore was cut by a human form. He
gathered up his gaze and withdrew it from the illimitable,
and lo, it was the lovely boy who crossed his vision coming
from the left along the sand. He was barefoot, ready for
wading, the slender legs uncovered above the knee, and
moved slowly, yet with such a proud, light tread as to make
it seem he had never worn shoes. He looked towards the
diagonal row of cabins; and the sight of the Russian family,

leading their lives there in joyous simplicity, distorted his features in a spasm of angry disgust. His brow darkened, his lips curled, one corner of the mouth was drawn down in a harsh line that marred the curve of the cheek, his frown was so heavy that the eyes seemed to sink in as they uttered beneath the black and vicious language of hate. He looked down, looked threateningly back once more; then giving it up with a violent and contemptuous shoulder-shrug, he left his enemies in the rear.

A feeling of delicacy, a qualm, almost like a sense of shame, made Aschenbach turn away as though he had not seen; he felt unwilling to take advantage of having been, by chance, privy to this passionate reaction. But he was in troth both moved and exhilarated – that is to say, he was delighted. This childish exhibition of fanaticism, directed against the good-naturedest simplicity in the world – it gave to the godlike and inexpressive the final human touch. The figure of the half-grown lad, a masterpiece from nature's own hand, had been significant enough when it gratified the eye alone; and now it evoked sympathy as well – the little episode had set it off, lent it a dignity in the onlooker's eyes that was beyond its years.

Aschenbach listened with still averted head to the boy's voice announcing his coming to his companions at the sand-heap. The voice was clear, though a little weak, but they answered, shouting his name – or his nickname – again and again. Aschenbach was not without curiosity to learn it, but could make out nothing more exact than two musical syll-ables, something like Adgio – or, often still, Adjiu, with a long-drawn-out *u* at the end. He liked the melodious sound, and found it fitting; said it over to himself a few times and turned back with satisfaction to his papers.

Holding his travelling-pad on his knees, he took his foun-tain-pen and began to answer various items of his correspond-ence. But presently he felt it too great a pity to turn his back, and the eyes of his mind, for the sake of mere commonplace correspondence, to this scene which was, after all, the most rewarding one he knew. He put aside his papers and swung round to the sea; in no long time, beguiled by the voices of the children at play, he had turned his head and sat resting it against the chair-back, while he gave himself up to contemplating the activities of the exquisite Adgio.

His eye found him at once, the red breast-knot was unmistakable. With some nine or ten companions, boys and girls of his own age and younger, he was busy putting in place an old plank to serve as a bridge across the ditches between the sandpiles. He directed the work by shouting and motioning with his head, and they were all chattering in many tongues – French, Polish, and even some of the Balkan languages. But his was the name oftenest on their lips, he was plainly sought after, wooed, admired. One lad in particular, a Pole like himself, with a name that sounded something like Jaschiu, a sturdy lad with brilliantined black hair, in a belted linen suit, was his particular liegeman and friend. Operations at the sand-pile being ended for the time, they two walked away along the beach, with their arms round each other's waists, and once the lad Jaschiu gave Adgio a kiss.

Aschenbach felt like shaking a finger at him. 'But you, Critobulus,' he thought with a smile, 'you I advise to take a year's leave. That long, at least, you will need for complete recovery.' A vendor came by with strawberries, and Aschenbach made his second breakfast of the great luscious, dead-ripe fruit. It had grown very warm, although the sun had not availed to pierce the heavy layer of mist. His mind felt relaxed, his senses revelled in this vast and soothing communion with the silence of the sea. The grave and serious man found sufficient occupation in speculating what name it could be that sounded like Adgio. And with the help of a few Polish memories he at length fixed on Tadzio, a shortened form of Thaddeus, which sounded, when called, like Tadziu or Adziu.

Tadzio was bathing. Aschenbach had lost sight of him for

a moment, then descried him far out in the water, which was shallow a very long way – saw his head, and his arm striking out like an oar. But his watchful family were already on the alert; the mother and governess called from the veranda in front of their bathing-cabin, until the lad's name, with its softened consonants and long-drawn *u*-sound, seemed to possess the beach like a rallying-cry; the cadence had something sweet and wild: 'Tadziu! Tadziu!' He turned and ran back against the water, churning the waves to a foam, his head flung high. The sight of this living figure, virginally pure and austere, with dripping locks, beautiful as a tender young god, emerging from the depths of sea and sky, outrunning the element – it conjured up mythologies, it was like a primeval legend, handed down from the beginning of time, of the birth of form, of the origin of the gods. With closed lids Aschenbach listened to this poesy hymning itself silently within him, and anon he thought it was good to be here and that he would stop awhile.

Afterwards Tadzio lay on the sand and rested from his bathe, wrapped in his white sheet, which he wore drawn underneath the right shoulder, so that his head was cradled on his bare right arm. And even when Aschenbach read, without looking up, he was conscious that the lad was there; that it would cost him but the slightest turn of the head to have the rewarding vision once more in his purview. Indeed, it was almost as though he sat there to guard the youth's repose; occupied, of course, with his own affairs, yet alive to the presence of that noble human creature close at hand. And his heart was stirred, it felt a father's kindness: such an emotion as the possessor of beauty can inspire in one who has offered himself up in spirit to create beauty.

At midday he left the beach, returned to the hotel, and was carried up in the lift to his room. There he lingered a little time before the glass and looked at his own grey hair, his keen and weary face. And he thought of his fame, and how people gazed respectfully at him in the streets, on account of his unerring gift of words and their power to charm. He called up all the worldly successes his genius had reaped, all he could remember, even his patent of nobility. Then went to luncheon down in the dining-room, sat at his little table and ate. Afterwards he mounted again in the lift, and a group of young folk, Tadzio among them, pressed with him into the little compartment. It was the first time Aschenbach had seen him close at hand, not merely in perspective, and could see and take account of the details of his humanity. Someone spoke to the lad, and he, answering, with indescribably lovely smile, stepped out again, as they had come to the first floor, backwards, with his eyes cast down. 'Beauty makes people self-conscious,' Aschenbach thought, and considered within himself imperatively why this should be. He had noted, further, that Tadzio's teeth were imperfect, rather jagged and bluish, without a healthy glaze, and of that peculiar brittle transparency which the teeth of chlorotic people often show. 'He is delicate, he is sickly,' Aschenbach thought. 'He will most likely not live to grow old.' He did not try to account for the pleasure the idea gave him.

In the afternoon he spent two hours in his room, then took the *vaporetto* to Venice, across the foul-smelling lagoon. He got out at San Marco, had his tea in the Piazza, and then, as his custom was, took a walk through the streets. But this walk of his brought about nothing less than a revolution in his mood and an entire change in all his plans.

There was a hateful sultriness in the narrow streets. The air was so heavy that all the manifold smells wafted out of houses, shops, and cook-shops – smells of oil, perfumery, and so forth – hung low, like exhalations, not dissipating. Cigarette smoke seemed to stand in the air, it drifted so slowly away. To-day the crowd in these narrow lanes oppressed the stroller instead of diverting him. The longer he walked, the more was he in tortures under that state, which is the product of the sea air and the sirocco and which excites and enervates at once. He perspired painfully. His eyes rebelled, his chest was heavy, he felt feverish, the blood throbbed in his temples. He fled from the huddled, narrow streets of the commercial city, crossed many bridges, and came into the poor quarter of Venice. Beggars waylaid him, the canals sickened him with their evil exhalations. He reached a quiet square, one of those that exist at the city's heart, forsaken of God and man; there he rested awhile on the margin of a fountain, wiped his brow, and admitted to himself that he must be gone.

For the second time, and now quite definitely, the city proved that in certain weathers it could be directly inimical to his health. Nothing but sheer unreasoning obstinacy would linger on, hoping for an unprophesiable change in the wind. A quick decision was in place. He could not go home at this stage, neither summer nor winter quarters would be ready. But Venice had not a monopoly of sea and shore: there were other spots where these were to be had without the evil concomitants of lagoon and fever-breeding vapours. He remembered a little bathing-place not far from Trieste of which he had had a good report. Why not go thither? At once, of course, in order that this second change might be worth the making. He resolved, he rose to his feet and sought the nearest gondola-landing, where he took a boat and was conveyed to San Marco through the gloomy windings of many canals, beneath balconies of delicate marble traceries flanked by carven lions; round slippery corners of wall, past melancholy façades with ancient business shields reflected in the rocking water. It was not too easy to arrive at his destination, for his gondolier, being in league with various lace-makers and glass-blowers, did his best to persuade his fare to pause, look, and be tempted to buy. Thus the charm of this bizarre passage through the heart of Venice, even while it played upon his spirit, yet was sensibly cooled by the predatory commercial spirit of the fallen queen of the seas.

Once back in his hotel, he announced at the office, even before dinner, that circumstances unforeseen obliged him to leave early next morning. The management expressed its regret, it changed his money and receipted his bill. He dined, and spent the luke-warm evening in a rocking-chair on the rear terrace, reading the newspapers. Before he went to bed, he made his luggage ready against the morning.

His sleep was not of the best, for the prospect of another journey made him restless. When he opened his window next morning, the sky was still overcast, but the air seemed fresher – and there and then his rue began. Had he not given notice too soon? Had he not let himself be swayed by a slight and momentary indisposition? If he had only been patient, not lost heart so quickly, tried to adapt himself to the climate, or even waited for a change in the weather before deciding! Then, instead of the hurry and flurry of departure, he would have before him now a morning like yesterday's on the beach. Too late! He must go on wanting what he had wanted yesterday. He dressed and at eight o'clock went down to breakfast.

When he entered the breakfast-room it was empty. Guests came in while he sat waiting for his order to be filled. As he sipped his tea he saw the Polish girls enter with their governess, chaste and morning-fresh, with sleep-reddened eyelids. They crossed the room and sat down at their table in the window. Behind them came the porter, cap in hand, to announce that it was time for him to go. The car was waiting to convey him and other travellers to the Hôtel Excelsior, whence they would go by motor-boat through the company's private canal to the station. Time pressed. But Aschenbach found it did nothing of the sort. There still lacked more than an hour of train-time. He felt irritated at the hotel habit of getting the guests out of the house earlier than necessary; and requested the porter to let him breakfast in peace. The man hesitated and withdrew, only to come back again five minutes later. The car could wait no longer. Good, then it might go, and take his trunk with it, Aschenbach answered with some heat. He would use the public conveyance, in his own time; he begged them to leave the choice of it to him. The functionary bowed. Aschenbach, pleased to be rid of him, made a leisurely meal, and even had a newspaper of the waiter. When at length he rose, the time was grown very short. And it so happened that at that moment Tadzio came through the glass doors into the room.

To reach his own table he crossed the traveller's path, and modestly cast down his eyes before the grey-haired man of the lofty brows – only to lift them again in that sweet way he had and direct his full soft gaze upon Aschenbach's face. Then he was past. 'For the last time, Tadzio,' thought the elder man. 'It was all too brief!' Quite unusually for him, he shaped a farewell with his lips, he actually uttered it, and added: 'May God bless you!' Then he went out, distributed tips, exchanged farewells with the mild little manager in the frock-coat, and, followed by the porter with his hand-luggage, left the hotel. On foot as he had come, he passed through the white-blossoming avenue, diagonally across the island to the boat-landing. He went on board at once – but the tale of his journey across the lagoon was a tale of woe, a passage through the very valley of regrets.

It was the well-known route: through the lagoon, past San Marco, up the Grand Canal. Aschenbach sat on the circular bench in the bows, with his elbow on the railing, one hand shading his eyes. They passed the Public Gardens, once more the princely charm of the Piazzetta rose up before him and then dropped behind, next came the great row of palaces, the canal curved, and the splendid marble arches of the Rialto came in sight. The traveller gazed – and his bosom was torn. The atmosphere of the city, the faintly rotten scent of swamp and sea, which had driven him to leave – in what deep, tender, almost painful draughts he breathed it in! How was it he had not known, had not thought, how much his heart was set upon it all! What this morning had been slight regret, some little doubt of his own wisdom, turned now to grief, to actual wretchedness, a mental agony so sharp that it repeatedly brought tears to his eyes, while he questioned himself how he could have foreseen it. The hardest part, the part that more than once it seemed he could not bear, was the thought that he should never more see Venice again. Since now for the second time the place had made him ill, since for the second time he had had to flee for his life, he must henceforth regard it as a forbidden spot, to be forever shunned; senseless to try it again, after he had proved himself unfit. Yes, if he fled it now, he felt that wounded pride must prevent his return to this spot where twice he had made actual bodily surrender. And this conflict between inclination and capacity all at once assumed, in this middle-aged man's mind, immense weight and importance; the physical defeat seemed a shameful thing, to be avoided at whatever cost; and he stood amazed at the ease with which on the day before he had yielded to it.

Meanwhile the steamer neared the station landing; his anguish of irresolution amounted almost to panic. To leave seemed to the sufferer impossible, to remain not less so. Torn thus between two alternatives, he entered the station. It was very late, he had not a moment to lose. Time pressed, it scourged him onward. He hastened to buy his ticket and looked round in the crowd to find the hotel porter. The man appeared and said that the trunk had already gone off. 'Gone already?' 'Yes, it has gone to Como.' 'To Como?' A hasty exchange of words – angry questions from Aschenbach, and puzzled replies from the porter – at length made it clear that the trunk had been put with the wrong luggage even before leaving the hotel, and in company with other trunks was now well on its way in precisely the wrong direction.

Aschenbach found it hard to wear the right expression as he heard this news. A reckless joy, a deep incredible mirthfulness shook him almost as with a spasm. The porter dashed off after the lost trunk, returning very soon, of course, to announce that his efforts were unavailing. Aschenbach said he would not travel without his luggage; that he would go back and wait at the Hôtel des Bains until it turned up. Was the company's motor-boat still outside? The man said yes, it was at the door. With his native eloquence he prevailed upon the ticket-agent to take back the ticket already purchased; he swore that he would wire, that no pains should be spared, that the trunk would be restored in the twinkling of an eye. And the unbelievable thing came to pass; the traveller, twenty minutes after he had reached the station, found himself once more on the Grand Canal on his way back to the Lido.

What a strange adventure indeed, this right-about face of destiny – incredible, humiliating, whimsical as any dream! To be passing again, within the hour, these scenes from which in profoundest grief he had but now taken leave forever! The little swift-moving vessel, a furrow of foam at its prow, tacking with droll agility between steamboats and gondolas, went like a shot to its goal; and he, its sole passenger, sat hiding the panic and thrills of a truant schoolboy beneath a mask of forced resignation. His breast still heaved from time to time with a burst of laughter over the contretemps. Things could not, he told himself, have fallen out more luckily. There would be the necessary explanations, a few astonished faces – then all would be well once more, a mischance prevented, a grievous error set right; and all he had thought to have left forever was his own once more, his for as long as he liked. . . . And did the boat's swift motion deceive him, or was the wind now coming from the sea?

The waves struck against the tiled sides of the narrow canal. At Hôtel Excelsior the automobile omnibus awaited the returned traveller and bore him along by the crisping waves back to the Hôtel des Bains. The little mustachioed manager in the frock-coat came down the steps to greet him.

In dulcet tones he deplored the mistake, said how painful

it was to the management and himself; applauded Aschenbach's resolve to stop on until the errant trunk came back; his former room, alas, was already taken, but another as good awaited his approval. '*Pas de chance, monsieur,*' said the Swiss lift-porter, with a smile, as he conveyed him upstairs. And the fugitive was soon quartered in another room which in situation and furnishings almost precisely resembled the first.

He laid out the contents of his hand-bag in their wonted places; then, tired out, dazed by the whirl of the extraordinary forenoon, subsided into the arm-chair by the open window. The sea wore a pale-green cast, the air felt thinner and purer, the beach with its cabins and boats had more colour, notwithstanding the sky was still grey. Aschenbach, his hands folded in his lap, looked out. He felt rejoiced to be back, yet displeased with his vacillating moods, his ignorance of his own real desires. Thus for nearly an hour he sat, dreaming, resting, barely thinking. At midday he saw Tadzio, in his striped sailor suit with red breast-knot, coming up from the sea, across the barrier and along the board walk to the hotel. Aschenbach recognized him, even at this height, knew it was he before he actually saw him, had it in mind to say to himself: 'Well, Tadzio, so here you are again too!' But the casual greeting died away before it reached his lips, slain by the truth in his heart. He felt the rapture of his blood, the poignant pleasure, and realized that it was for Tadzio's sake the leavetaking had been so hard.

He sat quite still, unseen at his high post, and looked within himself. His features were lively, he lifted his brows; a smile, alert, inquiring, vivid, widened the mouth. Then he raised his head, and with both hands, hanging limp over the chair-arms, he described a slow motion, palms outward, a lifting and turning movement, as though to indicate a wide embrace. It was a gesture of welcome, a calm and deliberate acceptance of what might come.

Now daily the naked god with cheeks aflame drove his four

fire-breathing steeds through heaven's spaces; and with him streamed the strong east wind that fluttered his yellow locks. A sheen, like white satin, lay over all the idly rolling sea's expanse. The sand was burning hot. Awnings of rust-coloured canvas were spanned before the bathing-huts, under the ether's quivering silver-blue; one spent the morning hours within the small, sharp square of shadow they purveyed. But evening too was rarely lovely: balsamic with the breath of flowers and shrubs from the near-by park, while overhead the constellations circled in their spheres, and the murmuring of the night-girded sea swelled softly up and whispered to the soul. Such nights as these contained the joyful promise of a sunlit morrow, brim-full of sweetly ordered idleness, studded thick with countless precious possibilities.

The guest detained here by so happy a mischance was far from finding the return of his luggage a ground for setting out anew. For two days he had suffered slight inconvenience and had to dine in the large salon in his travelling clothes. Then the lost trunk was set down in his room, and he hastened to unpack, filling presses and drawers with his possessions. He meant to stay on – and on; he rejoiced in the prospect of wearing a silk suit for the hot morning hours on the beach and appearing in acceptable evening dress at dinner.

He was quick to fall in with the pleasing monotony of this manner of life, readily enchanted by its mild soft brilliance and ease. And what a spot it is, indeed! – uniting the charms of a luxurious bathing-resort by a southern sea with the immediate nearness of a unique and marvellous city. Aschenbach was not pleasure-loving. Always, wherever and whenever it was the order of the day to be merry, to refrain from labour and make glad the heart, he would soon be conscious of the imperative summons – and especially was this so in his youth – back to the high fatigues, the sacred and fasting service that consumed his days. This spot and this alone had power to beguile him, to relax his resolution, to make him glad. At times

– of a forenoon perhaps, as he lay in the shadow of his awning, gazing out dreamily over the blue of the southern sea, or in the mildness of the night, beneath the wide starry sky, ensconced among the cushions of the gondola that bore him Lido-wards after an evening on the Piazza, while the gay lights faded and the melting music of the serenades died away on his ear – he would think of his mountain home, the theatre of his summer labours. There clouds hung low and trailed through the garden, violent storms extinguished the lights of the house at night, and the ravens he fed swung in the tops of the fir trees. And he would feel transported to Elysium, to the ends of the earth, to a spot most carefree for the sons of men, where no snow is, and no winter, no storms or downpours of rain; where Oceanus sends a mild and cooling breath, and days flow on in blissful idleness, without effort or struggle, entirely dedicate to the sun and the feasts of the sun.

Aschenbach saw the boy Tadzio almost constantly. The narrow confines of their world of hotel and beach, the daily round followed by all alike, brought him in close, almost uninterrupted touch with the beautiful lad. He encountered him everywhere – in the salons of the hotel, on the cooling rides to the city and back, among the splendours of the Piazza, and besides all this in many another going and coming as chance vouchsafed. But it was the regular morning hours on the beach which gave him his happiest opportunity to study and admire the lovely apparition. Yes, this immediate happiness, this daily recurring boon at the hand of circumstance, this it was that filled him with content, with joy in life, enriched his stay, and lingered out the row of sunny days that fell into place so pleasantly one behind the other.

He rose early – as early as though he had a panting press of work – and was among the first on the beach, when the sun was still benign and the sea dazzling white in its morning slumber. He gave the watchman a friendly good-morning and chatted with the barefoot, white-haired old man who prepared his place, spread the awning, trundled out the chair and table on to the little platform. Then he settled down; he had three or four hours before the sun reached its height and the fearful climax of its power; three or four hours while the sea went deeper and deeper blue; three or four hours in which to watch Tadzio.

He would see him coming up, on the left, along the margin of the sea; or from behind, between the cabins; or, with a start of joyful surprise, would discover that he himself was late, and Tadzio already down, in the blue and white bathing-suit that was now his only wear on the beach; there and engrossed in his usual activities in the sand, beneath the sun. It was a sweetly idle, trifling, fitful life, of play and rest, of strolling, wading, digging, fishing, swimming, lying on the sand. Often the women sitting on the platform would call out to him in their high voices: 'Tadziu! Tadziu!' and he would come running and waving his arms, eager to tell them what he had found, what caught – shells, seahorses, jelly-fish, and side-wards-running crabs. Aschenbach understood not a word he said; it might be the sheerest commonplace, in his ear it became mingled harmonies. Thus the lad's foreign birth raised his speech to music; a wanton sun showered splendour on him, and the noble distances of the sea formed the background which set off his figure.

Soon the observer knew every line and pose of this form that limned itself so freely against sea and sky; its every loveliness, though conned by heart, yet thrilled him each day afresh; his admiration knew no bounds, the delight of his eye was unending. Once the lad was summoned to speak to a guest who was waiting for his mother at their cabin. He ran up, ran dripping wet out of the sea, tossing his curls, and put out his hand, standing with his weight on one leg, resting the other foot on the toes; as he stood there in a posture of suspense the turn of his body was enchanting, while his features wore a look half shamefaced, half conscious of the duty breeding laid upon him to please. Or he would lie at full length, with his bath-robe around him, one slender young arm resting on the sand, his chin in the hollow of his hand; the lad they called Jaschiu squatting beside him, paying him court. There could be nothing lovelier on earth than the smile and look with which the playmate thus singled out rewarded his humble friend and vassal. Again, he might be at the water's edge, alone, removed from his family, quite close to Aschenbach; standing erect, his hands clasped at the back of his neck, rocking slowly on the balls of his feet, day-dreaming away into blue space, while little waves ran up and bathed his toes. The ringlets of honey-coloured hair clung to his temples and neck, the fine down along the upper vertebrae was yellow in the sunlight; the thin envelope of flesh covering the torso betrayed the delicate outlines of the ribs and the symmetry of the breast-structure. His armpits were still as smooth as a statue's, smooth the glistening hollows behind the knees, where the blue network of veins suggested that the body was formed of some stuff more transparent than mere flesh. What discipline, what precision of thought were expressed by the tense youthful perfection of this form! And yet the pure, strong will which had laboured in darkness and succeeded in bringing this godlike work of art to the light of day – was it not known and familiar to him, the artist? Was not the same force at work in himself when he strove in cold fury to liberate from the marble mass of language the slender forms of his art which he saw with the eye of his mind and would body forth to men as the mirror and image of spiritual beauty?

Mirror and image! His eyes took in the proud bearing of that figure there at the blue water's edge; with an outburst of rapture he told himself that what he saw was beauty's very essence; form as divine thought, the single and pure perfection which resides in the mind, of which an image and likeness, rare and holy, was here raised up for adoration. This was very frenzy – and without a scruple, nay, eagerly, the ageing artist

bade it come. His mind was in travail, his whole mental background in a state of flux. Memory flung up in him the primi-
tive thoughts which are youth's inheritance, but which with
him had remained latent, never leaping up into a blaze. Has
it not been written that the sun beguiles our attention from
things of the intellect to fix it on things of the sense? The sun,
they say, dazzles; so bewitching reason and memory that the
soul for very pleasure forgets its actual state, to cling with
doting on the loveliest of all the objects she shines on. Yes, and
then it is only through the medium of some corporeal being
that it can raise itself again to contemplation of higher things.
Amor, in sooth, is like the mathematician who in order to give
children a knowledge of pure form must do so in the language
of pictures; so, too, the god, in order to make visible the spirit,
avails himself of the forms and colours of human youth, gilding
it with all imaginable beauty that it may serve memory as a tool,
the very sight of which then sets us afire with pain and longing.

Such were the devotee's thoughts, such the power of his
emotions. And the sea, so bright with glancing sunbeams,
wove in his mind a spell and summoned up a lovely picture:
there was the ancient plane-tree outside the walls of Athens,
a hallowed, shady spot, fragrant with willow-blossom and
adorned with images and votive offerings in honour of the
nymphs and Achelous. Clear ran the smooth-pebbled stream
at the foot of the spreading tree. Crickets were fiddling. But
on the gentle grassy slope, where one could lie yet hold the
head erect, and shelter from the scorching heat, two men re-
clined, an elder with a younger, ugliness paired with beauty
and wisdom with grace. Here Socrates held forth to youthful
Phaedrus upon the nature of virtue and desire, wooing him
with insinuating wit and charming turns of phrase. He told
him of the shuddering and unwonted heat that comes upon him
whose heart is open, when his eye beholds an image of eternal
beauty; spoke of the impious and corrupt, who cannot conceive beauty though they see its image, and are incapable of

awe; and of the fear and reverence felt by the noble soul when he beholds a godlike face or a form which is a good image of beauty: how as he gazes he worships the beautiful one and scarcely dares to look upon him, but would offer sacrifice as to an idol or a god, did he not fear to be thought stark mad. 'For beauty, my Phaedrus, beauty alone, is lovely and visible at once. For, mark you, it is the sole aspect of the spiritual which we can perceive through our senses, or bear so to perceive. Else what should become of us, if the divine, if reason and virtue and truth, were to speak to us through the senses? Should we not perish and be consumed by love, as Semele aforetime was by Zeus? So beauty, then, is the beauty-lover's way to the spirit – but only the way, only the means, my little Phaedrus.' . . . And then, sly arch-lover that he was, he said the subtlest thing of all: that the lover was nearer the divine than the beloved; for the god was in the one but not in the other – perhaps the tenderest, most mocking thought that ever was thought, and source of all the guile and secret bliss the lover knows.

Thought that can emerge wholly into feeling, feeling that can merge wholly into thought – these are the artist's highest joy. And our solitary felt in himself at this moment power to command and wield a thought that thrilled with emotion, an emotion as precise and concentrated as thought: namely, that nature herself shivers with ecstasy when the mind bows down in homage before beauty. He felt a sudden desire to write. Eros, indeed, we are told, loves idleness, and for idle hours alone was he created. But in this crisis the violence of our sufferer's seizure was directed almost wholly towards production, its occasion almost a matter of indifference. News had reached him on his travels that a certain problem had been raised, the intellectual world challenged for its opinion on a great and burning question of art and taste. By nature and experience the theme was his own: and he could not resist the temptation to set it off in the glistering foil of his words. He would write, and moreover he would write in Tadzio's presence. This lad should be in a sense his model, his style should follow the lines of this figure that seemed to him divine; he would snatch up this beauty into the realms of the mind, as once the eagle bore the Trojan shepherd aloft. Never had the pride of the word been so sweet to him, never had he known so well that Eros is in the word, as in those perilous and precious hours when he sat at his rude table, within the shade of his awning, his idol full in his view and the music of his voice in his ears, and fashioned his little essay after the model Tadzio's beauty set: that page and a half of choicest prose, so chaste, so lofty, so poignant with feeling, which would shortly be the wonder and admiration of the multitude. Verily it is well for the world that it sees only the beauty of the completed work and not its origins nor the conditions whence it sprang; since knowledge of the artist's inspiration might often but confuse and alarm and so prevent the full effect of its excellence. Strange hours, indeed, these were, and strangely unnerving the labour that filled them! Strangely fruitful intercourse this, between one body and another mind! When Aschenbach put aside his work and left the beach he felt exhausted, he felt broken – conscience reproached him, as it were after a debauch.

Next morning on leaving the hotel he stood at the top of the stairs leading down from the terrace and saw Tadzio in front of him on his way to the beach. The lad had just reached the gate in the railings, and he was alone. Aschenbach felt, quite simply, a wish to overtake him, to address him and have the pleasure of his reply and answering look; to put upon a blithe and friendly footing his relation with this being who all unconsciously had so greatly heightened and quickened his emotions. The lovely youth moved at a loitering pace – he might be easily overtaken; and Aschenbach hastened his own step. He reached him on the board walk that ran behind the bathing-cabins, and all but put out his hand to lay it on shoulder or head, while his lips parted to utter a friendly salutation in French. But – perhaps from the swift pace of his last few steps – he found his heart throbbing unpleasantly fast, while his breath came in such quick pants that he could only have gasped had he tried to speak. He hesitated, sought after self-control, was suddenly panic-stricken lest the boy notice him hanging there behind him and look round. Then he gave up, abandoned his plan, and passed him with bent head and hurried step.

'Too late! Too late!' he thought as he went by. But was it too late? This step he had delayed to take might so easily have put everything in a lighter key, have led to a sane recovery from his folly. But the truth may have been that the ageing man did not want to be cured, that his illusion was far too dear to him. Who shall unriddle the puzzle of the artist nature? Who understands that mingling of discipline and licence in which it stands so deeply rooted? For not to be able to want sobriety is licentious folly. Aschenbach was no longer disposed to self-analysis. He had no taste for it; his self-esteem, the attitude of mind proper to his years, his maturity and single-mindedness, disinclined him to look within himself and decide whether it was constraint or puerile sensuality that had prevented him from carrying out his project. He felt confused, he was afraid someone, if only the watchman, might have been observing his behaviour and final surrender – very much he feared being ridiculous. And all the time he was laughing at himself for his serio-comic seizure. 'Quite crestfallen,' he thought. 'I was like the gamecock that lets his wings droop in the battle. That must be the Love-God himself, that makes us hang our heads at sight of beauty and weighs our proud spirits low as the ground.' Thus he played with the idea – he embroidered upon it, and was too arrogant to admit fear of an emotion.

The term he had set for his holiday passed by unheeded; he had no thought of going home. Ample funds had been sent him. His sole concern was that the Polish family might leave and a chance question put to the hotel barber elicited the information that they had come only very shortly before himself. The sun browned his face and hands, the invigorating salty air heightened his emotional energies. Heretofore he had wont to give out at once, in some new effort, the powers accumulated by sleep or food or outdoor air; but now the strength that flowed in upon him with each day of sun and sea and idleness he let go up in one extravagant gush of emotional intoxication.

His sleep was fitful; the priceless, equable days were divided one from the next by brief nights filled with happy unrest. He went, indeed, early to bed, for at nine o'clock, with the departure of Tadzio from the scene, the day was over for him. But in the faint greyness of the morning a tender pang would go through him as his heart was minded of its adventure; he could no longer bear his pillow and rising, would wrap himself against the early chill and sit down by the window to await the sunrise. Awe of the miracle filled his soul new-risen from its sleep. Heaven, earth, and its waters yet lay enfolded in the ghostly, glassy pallor of dawn; one paling star still swam in the shadowy vast. But there came a breath, a winged word from far and inaccessible abodes, that Eos was rising from the side of her spouse, and there was that first sweet reddening of the farthest strip of sea and sky that manifests creation to man's sense. She neared, the goddess, ravisher of youth, who stole away Cleitos and Cephalus and, defying all the envious Olympians, tasted beautiful Orion's love. At the world's edge began a strewing of roses, a shining and a blooming ineffably pure; baby cloudlets hung illuminated, like attendant amoretti, in the blue and blushful haze; purple effulgence fell upon the sea, that seemed to heave it forward on its welling waves; from horizon to zenith went quivering thrusts like golden lances, the gleam became a glare; without a sound, with godlike violence, glow and glare and rolling flames streamed upwards, and with flying hoof-beats the steeds of the sun-god mounted the sky. The lonely watcher sat, the splendour of the god shone on him, he closed his eyes and let the glory kiss his lids. Forgotten feelings, precious pangs of his youth, quenched long since by the stern service that had been his life and now returned so strangely metamorphosed – he recognized them with a puzzled, wondering smile. He mused, he dreamed, his lips slowly shaped a name; still smiling, his face turned seawards and his hands lying folded in his lap, he fell asleep once more as he sat.

But that day, which began so fierily and festally, was not like other days; it was transmuted and gilded with mythical significance. For whence could come the breath, so mild and meaningful, like a whisper from higher spheres, that played about temple and ear? Troops of small feathery white clouds ranged over the sky, like grazing herds of the gods. A stronger wind arose, and Poseidon's horses ran up, arching their manes, among them too the steers of him with the purpled locks, who lowered their horns and bellowed as they came on; while like prancing goats the waves on the farther strand leaped among the craggy rocks. It was a world possessed, peopled by Pan, that closed round the spellbound man, and his doting heart conceived the most delicate fancies. When the sun was going down behind Venice, he would sometimes sit on a bench in the park and watch Tadzio, white-clad, with gay-coloured sash, at play there on the rolled gravel with his ball; and at such times it was not Tadzio whom he saw, but Hyacinthus, doomed to die because two gods were rivals for his love. Ah, yes, he tasted the envious pangs that Zephyr knew when his rival, bow and cithara, oracle and all forgot, played with the beauteous youth; he watched the discus, guided by torturing jealousy, strike the beloved head; paled as he received the broken body in his arms, and saw the flower spring up, watered by that sweet blood and signed for evermore with his lament.

There can be no relation more strange, more critical, than that between two beings who know each other only with their eyes, who meet daily, yes, even hourly, eye each other with a fixed regard, and yet by some whim or freak of convention feel constrained to act like strangers. Uneasiness rules between them, unslaked curiosity, a hysterical desire to give rein to their suppressed impulse to recognize and address each other; even, actually, a sort of strained but mutual regard. For one human being instinctively feels respect and love for another human being so long as he does not know him well enough to judge him; and that he does not, the craving he feels is evidence.

Some sort of relationship and acquaintanceship was perforce set up between Aschenbach and the youthful Tadzio; it was with a thrill of joy the older man perceived that the lad was not entirely unresponsive to all the tender notice lavished on him. For instance, what should move the lovely youth, nowadays when he descended to the beach, always to avoid the board walk behind the bathing-huts and saunter along the sand, passing Aschenbach's tent in front, sometimes so unnecessarily close as almost to graze his table or chair? Could the power of an emotion so beyond his own so draw, so fascinate its innocent object? Daily Aschenbach would wait for Tadzio. Then sometimes, on his approach, he would pretend to be preoccupied and let the charmer pass unregarded by. But sometimes he looked up, and their glances met; when that happened both were profoundly serious. The elder's dignified and cultured mien let nothing appear of his inward state; but in Tadzio's eyes a question lay – he faltered in his step, gazed on the ground, then up again with that ineffably sweet look he had; and when he was past, something in his bearing seemed to say that only good breeding hindered him from turning round.

But once, one evening, it fell out differently. The Polish brother and sisters, with their governess, had missed the evening meal, and Aschenbach had noted the fact with concern. He was restive over their absence, and after dinner walked

up and down in front of the hotel, in evening dress and a straw
hat; when suddenly he saw the nunlike sisters with their companion appear in the light of the arc-lamps, and four paces
behind them Tadzio. Evidently they came from the steamer-
landing, having dined for some reason in Venice. It had been
chilly on the lagoon, for Tadzio wore a dark-blue reefer-
jacket with gilt buttons, and a cap to match. Sun and sea
air could not burn his skin, it was the same creamy marble
hue as at first - though he did look a little pale, either from
the cold or in the bluish moonlight of the arc-lamps. The
shapely brows were so delicately drawn, the eyes so deeply
dark – lovelier he was than words could say, and as often the
thought visited Aschenbach, and brought its own pang, that
language could but extol, not reproduce, the beauties of the
sense.

The sight of that dear form was unexpected, it had appeared
unhoped-for, without giving him time to compose his features.
Joy, surprise, and admiration might have painted themselves
quite openly upon his face – and just at this second it happened
that Tadzio smiled. Smiled at Aschenbach, unabashed and
friendly, a speaking, winning, captivating smile, with slowly
parting lips. With such a smile it might be that Narcissus bent
over the mirroring pool, a smile profound, infatuated, lingering, as he put out his arms to the reflection of his own beauty;
the lips just slightly pursed, perhaps half-realizing his own
folly in trying to kiss the cold lips of his shadow – with a
mingling of coquetry and curiosity and a faint unease, enthrall-
ing and enthralled.

Aschenbach received that smile and turned away with it as
though entrusted with a fatal gift. So shaken was he that he
had to flee from the lighted terrace and front gardens and seek
out with hurried steps the darkness of the park at the rear.
Reproaches strangely mixed of tenderness and remonstrance
burst from him: 'How dare you smile like that! No one is
allowed to smile like that!' He flung himself on a bench, his

composure gone to the winds, and breathed in the nocturnal fragrance of the garden. He leaned back, with hanging arms, quivering from head to foot, and quite unmanned he whispered the hackneyed phrase of love and longing – impossible in these circumstances, absurd, abject, ridiculous enough, yet sacred too, and not unworthy of honour even here: 'I love you!'

In the fourth week of his stay on the Lido, Gustave von Aschenbach made certain singular observations touching the world about him. He noticed, in the first place, that though the season was approaching its height, yet the number of guests declined and, in particular, that the German tongue had suffered a rout, being scarcely or never heard in the land. At table and on the beach he caught nothing but foreign words. One day at the barber's – where he was now a frequent visitor – he heard something rather startling. The barber mentioned a German family who had just left the Lido after a brief stay, and rattled on in his obsequious way: 'The signore is not leaving – he has no fear of the sickness, has he?' Aschenbach looked at him. 'The sickness?' he repeated. Whereat the prattler fell silent, became very busy all at once, affected not to hear. When Aschenbach persisted he said he really knew nothing at all about it, and tried in a fresh burst of eloquence to drown the embarrassing subject.

That was one forenoon. After luncheon, Aschenbach had himself ferried across to Venice, in a dead calm, under a burning sun; driven by his mania, he was following the Polish young folk, whom he had seen with their companion, taking the way to the landing-stage. He did not find his idol on the Piazza. But as he sat there at tea, at a little round table on the shady side, suddenly he noticed a peculiar odour, which, it seemed to him now, had been in the air for days without his being aware: a sweetish, medicinal smell, associated with wounds and disease and suspect cleanliness. He sniffed and pondered and at length recognized it; finished his tea and left the square at the end facing the cathedral. In the narrow space the stench grew stronger. At the street corners placards were stuck up, in which the city authorities warned the population against the danger of certain infections of the gastric system, prevalent during the heated season; advising them not to eat oysters or other shell-fish and not to use the canal waters. The ordinance showed every sign of minimizing an existing situation. Little groups of people stood about silently in the squares and on the bridges; the traveller moved among them, watched and listened and thought.

He spoke to a shopkeeper lounging at his door among dangling coral necklaces and trinkets of artificial amethyst, and asked him about the disagreeable odour. The man looked at him, heavy-eyed, and hastily pulled himself together. 'Just a formal precaution, signore,' he said, with a gesture. 'A police regulation we have to put up with. The air is sultry – the sirocco is not wholesome, as the signore knows. Just a precautionary measure, you understand – probably unnecessary. . . .' Aschenbach thanked him and passed on. And on the boat that bore him back to the Lido he smelt the germicide again.

On reaching his hotel he sought the table in the lobby and buried himself in the newspapers. The foreign-language sheets had nothing. But in the German papers certain rumours were mentioned, statistics given, then officially denied, then the good faith of the denials called in question. The departure of the German and Austrian contingent was thus made plain. As for other nationals, they knew or suspected nothing – they were still undisturbed. Aschenbach tossed the newspapers back on the table. 'It ought to be kept quiet,' he thought, aroused. 'It should not be talked about.' And he felt in his heart a curious elation at these events impending in the world about him. Passion is like crime: it does not thrive on the established order and the common round; it welcomes every blow dealt the bourgeois structure, every weakening of the social fabric, because therein it feels a sure hope of its own advantage. These things that were going on in the unclean alleys of Venice, under cover of an official hushing-up policy – they gave Aschenbach a dark satisfaction. The city's evil secret mingled with the one in the depths of his heart – and he would have staked all he possessed to keep it, since in his infatuation he cared for nothing but to keep Tadzio here, and owned to himself, not without horror, that he could not exist were the lad to pass from his sight.

He was no longer satisfied to owe his communion with his charmer to chance and the routine of hotel life; he had begun to follow and waylay him. On Sundays, for example, the Polish family never appeared on the beach. Aschenbach guessed they went to mass at San Marco and pursued them thither. He passed from the glare of the Piazza into the golden twilight of the holy place and found him he sought bowed in worship over a prie-dieu. He kept in the background, standing on the fissured mosaic pavement among the devout populace, that knelt and muttered and made the sign of the cross; and the crowded splendour of the oriental temple weighed voluptuously on his sense. A heavily ornate priest intoned and gesticulated before the altar, where little candle-flames flickered helplessly in the reek of incense-breathing smoke; and with that cloying sacrificial smell another seemed to mingle – the odour of the sickened city. But through all the glamour and glitter, Aschenbach saw the exquisite creature there in front turn his head, seek out and meet his lover's eye.

The crowd streamed out through the portals into the brilliant square thick with fluttering doves, and the fond fool stood aside in the vestibule on the watch. He saw the Polish family leave the church. The children took ceremonial leave of their mother, and she turned towards the Piazzetta on her way home, while his charmer and the cloistered sisters, with their governess, passed beneath the clock tower into the

Merceria. When they were a few paces on, he followed – he
stole behind them on their walk through the city. When they
paused, he did so too; when they turned round, he fled into
inns and courtyards to let them pass. Once he lost them from
view, hunted feverishly over bridges and in filthy *culs-de-sac*,
only to confront them suddenly in a narrow passage whence
there was no escape, and experience a moment of panic fear.
Yet it would be untrue to say he suffered. Mind and heart
were drunk with passion, his footsteps guided by the daemonic
power whose pastime it is to trample on human reason and
dignity.

Tadzio and his sisters at length took a gondola. Aschenbach
hid behind a portico or fountain while they embarked and
directly they pushed off did the same. In a furtive whisper he
told the boatman he would tip him well to follow at a little
distance the other gondola, just rounding a corner, and fairly
sickened at the man's quick, sly grasp and ready acceptance
of the go-between's role.

Leaning back among soft, black cushions he swayed gently
in the wake of the other black-snouted bark, to which the
strength of his passion chained him. Sometimes it passed from
his view, and then he was assailed by an anguish of unrest.
But his guide appeared to have long practice in affairs like
these; always, by dint of short cuts or deft manoeuvres, he
contrived to overtake the coveted sight. The air was heavy and
foul, the sun burnt down through a slate-coloured haze.
Water slapped gurgling against wood and stone. The gondolier's cry, half warning, half salute, was answered with
singular accord from far within the silence of the labyrinth.
They passed little gardens high up the crumbling wall, hung
with clustering white and purple flowers that sent down an
odour of almonds. Moorish lattices showed shadowy in the
gloom. The marble steps of a church descended into the canal,
and on them a beggar squatted, displaying his misery to view,
showing the whites of his eyes, holding out his hat for alms.

Farther on a dealer in antiquities cringed before his lair, inviting the passer-by to enter and be duped. Yes, this was Venice, this the fair frailty that fawned and that betrayed, half fairy-tale, half snare; the city in whose stagnating air the art of painting once put forth so lusty a growth, and where musicians were moved to accords so weirdly lulling and lascivious. Our adventurer felt his senses wooed by this voluptuousness of sight and sound, tasted his secret knowledge that the city sickened and hid its sickness for love of gain, and bent an ever more unbridled leer on the gondola that glided on before him.

It came at last to this – that his frenzy left him capacity for nothing else but to pursue his flame; to dream of him absent, to lavish, loverlike, endearing terms on his mere shadow. He was alone, he was a foreigner, he was sunk deep in this belated bliss of his – all which enabled him to pass unblushing through experiences well-nigh unbelievable. One night, returning late from Venice, he paused by his beloved's chamber door in the second storey, leaned his head against the panel, and remained there long, in utter drunkenness, powerless to tear himself away, blind to the danger of being caught in so mad an attitude.

And yet there were not wholly lacking moments when he paused and reflected, when in consternation he asked himself what path was this on which he had set his foot. Like most other men of parts and attainments, he had an aristocratic interest in his forbears, and when he achieved a success he liked to think he had gratified them, compelled their admiration and regard. He thought of them now, involved as he was in this illicit adventure, seized of these exotic excesses of feeling; thought of their stern self-command and decent manliness, and gave a melancholy smile. What would they have said? What, indeed, would they have said to his entire life, that varied to the point of degeneracy from theirs? This life in the bonds of art, had not he himself, in the days of his youth and in the very spirit of those bourgeois forefathers, pronounced mocking judgement upon it? And yet, at bottom, it had been so like their own! It had been a service, and he a soldier, like some of them; and art was war – a grilling, exhausting struggle that nowadays wore one out before one could grow old. It had been a life of self-conquest, a life against odds, dour, steadfast, abstinent; he had made it symbolical of the kind of over-strained heroism the time admired, and he was entitled to call it manly, even courageous. He wondered if such a life might not be somehow specially pleasing in the eyes of the god who had him in his power. For Eros had received most countenance among the most valiant nations – yes, were we not told that in their cities prowess made him flourish exceedingly? And many heroes of olden time had willingly borne his yoke, not counting any humiliation such as if it happened by the god's decree; vows, prostrations, self-abasements, these were no source of shame to the lover; rather they reaped him praise and honour.

Thus did the fond man's folly condition his thoughts; thus did he seek to hold his dignity upright in his own eyes. And all the while he kept doggedly on the traces of the disreputable secret the city kept hidden at its heart, just as he kept his own – and all that he learned fed his passion with vague, lawless hopes. He turned over newspapers at cafés, bent on finding a report on the progress of the disease; and in the German sheets, which had ceased to appear on the hotel table, he found a series of contradictory statements. The deaths, it was variously asserted, ran to twenty, to forty, to a hundred or more; yet in the next day's issue the existence of the pestilence was, if not roundly denied, reported as a matter of a few sporadic cases such as might be brought into a seaport town. After that the warnings would break out again, and the protests against the unscrupulous game the authorities were playing. No definite information was to be had.

And yet our solitary felt he had a sort of first claim on a

share in the unwholesome secret; he took a fantastic satisfaction in putting leading questions to such persons as were interested to conceal it, and forcing them to explicit untruths by way of denial. One day he attacked the manager, that small, soft-stepping man in the French frock-coat, who was moving about among the guests at luncheon, supervising the service and making himself socially agreeable. He paused at Aschenbach's table to exchange a greeting, and the guest put a question, with a negligent, casual air: 'Why in the world are they forever disinfecting the city of Venice?' 'A police regulation,' the adroit one replied; 'a precautionary measure, intended to protect the health of the public during this unseasonably warm and sultry weather.' 'Very praiseworthy of the police.' Aschenbach gravely responded. After a further exchange of meteorological commonplaces the manager passed on.

It happened that a band of street musicians came to perform in the hotel gardens that evening after dinner. They grouped themselves beneath an iron stanchion supporting an arc-light, two women and two men, and turned their faces, that shone white in the glare, up towards the guests who sat on the hotel terrace enjoying this popular entertainment along with their coffee and iced drinks. The hotel lift-boys, waiters, and office staff stood in the doorway and listened; the Russian family displayed the usual Russian absorption in their enjoyment – they had their chairs put down into the garden to be nearer the singers and sat there in a half-circle with gratitude painted on their features, the old serf in her turban erect behind their chairs.

These strolling players were adepts at mandolin, guitar, harmonica, even compassing a reedy violin. Vocal numbers alternated with instrumental, the younger woman, who had a high, shrill voice, joining in a love-duet with the sweetly falsettoing tenor. The actual head of the company, however, and incontestably its most gifted member, was the other man,

c

who played the guitar. He was a sort of baritone buffo; with
no voice to speak of, but possessed of a pantomimic gift and
remarkable burlesque *élan*. Often he stepped out of the group
and advanced towards the terrace, guitar in hand, and his
audience rewarded his sallies with bursts of laughter. The
Russians in their parterre seats were beside themselves with
delight over this display of southern vivacity; their shouts and
screams of applause encouraged him to bolder and bolder
flights.

Aschenbach sat near the balustrade, a glass of pomegranate-
juice and soda-water sparkling ruby-red before him, with
which he now and then moistened his lips. His nerves drank
in thirstily the unlovely sounds, the vulgar and sentimental
tunes, for passion paralyses good taste and makes its victim
accept with rapture what a man in his senses would either
laugh at or turn from with disgust. Idly he sat and watched
the antics of the buffoon with his face set in a fixed and painful smile, while inwardly his whole being was rigid with the
intensity of the regard he bent on Tadzio, leaning over the
railing six paces off.

He lounged there, in the white belted suit he sometimes
wore at dinner, in all his innate, inevitable grace, with his left
arm on the balustrade, his legs crossed, the right hand on the
supporting hip; and looked down on the strolling singers with
an expression that was hardly a smile, but rather a distant
curiosity and polite toleration. Now and then he straightened
himself and with a charming movement of both arms drew
down his white blouse through his leather belt, throwing out
his chest. And sometimes – Aschenbach saw it with triumph,
with horror, and a sense that his reason was tottering – the lad
would cast a glance, that might be slow and cautious, or might
be sudden and swift, as though to take him by surprise, to the
place where his lover sat. Aschenbach did not meet the glance.
An ignoble caution made him keep his eyes in leash. For in
the rear of the terrace sat Tadzio's mother and governess; and

matters had gone so far that he feared to make himself con-
spicuous. Several times, on the beach, in the hotel lobby, on
the Piazza, he had seen, with a stealing numbness, that they
called Tadzio away from his neighbourhood. And his pride
revolted at the affront, even while conscience told him it was
deserved.

The performer below presently began a solo, with guitar
accompaniment, a street song in several stanzas, just then the
rage all over Italy. He delivered it in a striking and dramatic
recitative, and his company joined in the refrain. He was a
man of slight build, with a thin, undernourished face; his
shabby felt hat rested on the back of his neck, a great mop of
red hair sticking out in front; and he stood there on the gravel
in advance of his troupe, in an impudent, swaggering posture,
twanging the strings of his instrument and flinging a witty
and rollicking recitative up to the terrace, while the veins on
his forehead swelled with the violence of his effort. He was
scarcely a Venetian type, belonging rather to the race of
Neapolitan jesters, half bully, half comedian, brutal, blustering,
an unpleasant customer, and entertaining to the last degree.
The words of his song were trivial and silly, but on his lips,
accompanied with gestures of head, hands, arms, and body,
with leers and winks and the loose play of the tongue in the
corner of his mouth, they took on meaning; an equivocal
meaning, yet vaguely offensive. He wore a white sports shirt
with a suit of ordinary clothes, and a strikingly large and
naked-looking Adam's apple rose out of the open collar.
From that pale, snub-nosed face it was hard to judge of his
age; vice sat on it, it was furrowed with grimacing, and two
deep wrinkles of defiance and self-will, almost of desperation,
stood oddly between the red brows, above the grinning
mobile mouth. But what more than all drew upon him the
profound scrutiny of our solitary watcher was that this suspicious figure seemed to carry with it its own suspicious
odour. For whenever the refrain occurred and the singer, with

waving arms and antic gestures, passed in his grotesque march immediately beneath Aschenbach's seat, a strong smell of carbolic was wafted up to the terrace.

After the song he began to take up money, beginning with the Russian family, who gave liberally, and then mounting the steps to the terrace. But here he became as cringing as he had before been forward. He glided between the tables, bowing and scraping, showing his strong white teeth in a servile smile, though the two deep furrows on the brow were still very marked. His audience looked at the strange creature as he went about collecting his livelihood, and their curiosity was not unmixed with disfavour. They tossed coins with their finger-tips into his hat and took care not to touch it. Let the enjoyment be never so great, a sort of embarrassment always comes when the comedian oversteps the physical distance between himself and respectable people. This man felt it and sought to make his peace by fawning. He came along the railing to Aschenbach, and with him came that smell no one else seemed to notice.

'Listen!' said the solitary, in a low voice, almost mechanically; 'they are disinfecting Venice – why?' The mountebank answered hoarsely: 'Because of the police. Orders, signore. On account of the heat and the sirocco. The sirocco is oppressive. Not good for the health.' He spoke as though surprised that anyone could ask, and with the flat of his hand he demonstrated how oppressive the sirocco was. 'So there is no plague in Venice?' Aschenbach asked the question between his teeth, very low. The man's expressive face fell, he put on a look of comical innocence. 'A plague? What sort of plague? Is the sirocco a plague? Or perhaps our police are a plague! You are making fun of us, signore! A plague! Why should there be? The police make regulations on account of the heat and the weather. . . .' He gestured. 'Quite,' said Aschenbach, once more, soft and low; and dropping an unduly large coin into the man's hat dismissed him with a sign. He bowed very low and left. But he had not reached the steps when two of the hotel servants flung themselves on him and began to whisper, their faces close to his. He shrugged, seemed to be giving assurances, to be swearing he had said nothing. It was not hard to guess the import of his words. They let him go at last and he went back into the garden, where he conferred briefly with his troupe and then stepped forward for a farewell song.

It was one Aschenbach had never to his knowledge heard before, a rowdy air, with words in impossible dialect. It had a laughing-refrain in which the other three artists joined at the top of their lungs. The refrain had neither words nor accompaniment, it was nothing but rhythmical, modulated, natural laughter, which the soloist in particular knew how to render with most deceptive realism. Now that he was farther off his audience, his self-assurance had come back, and this laughter of his rang with a mocking note. He would be overtaken, before he reached the end of the last line of each stanza; he would catch his breath, lay his hand over his mouth, his voice would quaver and his shoulders shake, he would lose power to contain himself longer. Just at the right moment each time, it came whooping, bawling, crashing out of him, with a verisimilitude that never failed to set his audience off in profuse and unpremeditated mirth that seemed to add gusto to his own. He bent his knees, he clapped his thigh, he held his sides, he looked ripe for bursting. He no longer laughed, but yelled, pointing his finger at the company there above as though there could be in all the world nothing so comic as they; until at last they laughed in hotel, terrace, and garden, down to the waiters, lift-boys, and servants – laughed as though possessed.

Aschenbach could no longer rest in his chair, he sat poised for flight. But the combined effect of the laughing, the hospital odour in his nostrils, and the nearness of the beloved was to hold him in a spell; he felt unable to stir. Under cover of the general commotion he looked across at Tadzio and saw that the lovely boy returned his gaze with a seriousness that seemed the copy of his own; the general hilarity, it seemed to say, had no power over him, he kept aloof. The grey-haired man was overpowered, disarmed by this docile, childlike deference; with difficulty he refrained from hiding his face in his hands. Tadzio's habit, too, of drawing himself up and taking a deep sighing breath struck him as being due to an oppression of the chest. 'He is sickly, he will never live to grow up,' he thought once again, with that dispassionate vision to which his madness of desire sometimes so strangely gave way. And compassion struggled with the reckless exultation of his heart.

The players, meanwhile, had finished and gone; their leader bowing and scraping, kissing his hands and adorning his leave-taking with antics that grew madder with the applause they evoked. After all the others were outside, he pretended to run backwards full tilt against a lamp-post and slunk to the gate apparently doubled over with pain. But there he threw off his buffoon's mask, stood erect, with an elastic straightening of his whole figure, ran out his tongue impudently at the guests on the terrace, and vanished in the night. The company dispersed. Tadzio had long since left the balustrade. But he, the lonely man, sat for long, to the waiters' great annoyance, before the dregs of pomegranate-juice in his glass. Time passed, the night went on. Long ago, in his parental home, he had watched the sand filter through an hour-glass – he could still see, as though it stood before him, the fragile, pregnant little toy. Soundless and fine the rust-red streamlet ran through the narrow neck and made, as it declined in the upper cavity, an exquisite little vortex.

The very next afternoon the solitary took another step in pursuit of his fixed policy of baiting the outer world. This time he had all possible success. He went, that is, into the English travel bureau in the Piazza, changed some money at the desk, and posing as the suspicious foreigner, put his fateful question. The clerk was a tweed-clad young Britisher, with his eyes set close together, his hair parted in the middle, and radiating that steady reliability which makes his like so strange a phenomenon in the *gamin*, agile-witted south. He began: 'No ground for alarm, sir. A mere formality. Quite regular in view of the unhealthy climatic conditions.' But then, looking up, he chanced to meet with his own blue eyes the stranger's weary, melancholy gaze, fixed on his face. The Englishman coloured. He continued in a lower voice, rather confused: 'At least, that is the official explanation, which they see fit to stick to. I may tell you there's a bit more to it than that.' And then, in his good, straightforward way, he told the truth.

For the past several years Asiatic cholera had shown a strong tendency to spread. Its source was the hot, moist swamps of the delta of the Ganges, where it bred in the mephitic air of that primeval island-jungle, among whose bamboo thickets the tiger crouches, where life of every sort flourishes in rankest abundance, and only man avoids the spot. Thence the pestilence had spread throughout Hindustan, ranging with great violence; moved eastwards to China, westward to Afghanistan and Persia; following the great caravan routes, it brought terror to Astrakhan, terror to Moscow. Even while Europe trembled lest the spectre be seen striding westward across country, it was carried by sea from Syrian ports and appeared simultaneously at several points on the Mediterranean littoral; raised its head in Toulon and Malaga, Palermo and Naples, and soon got a firm hold in Calabria and Apulia. Northern Italy had been spared – so far. But in May the horrible vibrios were found on the same day in two bodies: the emaciated, blackened corpses of a bargee and a woman who kept a green-grocer's shop. Both cases were hushed up. But in a week there were ten more – twenty, thirty in different quarters of the town. An Austrian provincial, having come to Venice on a few days' pleasure trip, went home and died with all the symptoms of the plague. Thus was explained the fact that the

German-language papers were the first to print the news of the Venetian outbreak. The Venetian authorities published in reply a statement to the effect that the state of the city's health had never been better; at the same time instituting the most necessary precautions. But by that time the food supplies – milk, meat, or vegetables – had probably been contaminated, for death unseen and unacknowledged was devouring and laying waste in the narrow streets, while a brooding, unseasonable heat warmed the waters of the canals and encouraged the spread of the pestilence. Yes, the disease seemed to flourish and wax strong, to redouble its generative powers. Recoveries were rare. Eighty out of every hundred died, and horribly, for the onslaught was of the extremest violence, and not infrequently of the 'dry' type, the most malignant form of the contagion. In this form the victim's body loses power to expel the water secreted by the blood-vessels, it shrivels up, he passes with hoarse cries from convulsion to convulsion, his blood grows thick like pitch and he suffocates in a few hours. He is fortunate indeed, if, as sometimes happens, the disease, after a slight *malaise*, takes the form of a profound unconsciousness, from which the sufferer seldom or never rouses. By the beginning of June the quarantine buildings of the *ospedale civico* had quietly filled up, the two orphan asylums were entirely occupied, and there was a hideously brisk traffic between the *Nuovo Fundamento* and the island of San Michele, where the cemetery was. But the city was not swayed by high-minded motives or regard for international agreements. The authorities were more actuated by fear of being out of pocket, by regard for the new exhibition of paintings just opened in the Public Gardens, or by apprehension of the large losses the hotels and the shops that catered to foreigners would suffer in case of panic and blockade. And the fears of the people supported the persistent official policy of silence and denial. The city's first medical officer, an honest and competent man, had indignantly resigned his office and been privily replaced by a more compliant person. The fact was known; and this corruption in high places played its part, together with the suspense as to where the walking terror might strike next, to demoralize the baser elements in the city and encourage those antisocial forces which shun the light of day. There was intemperance, indecency, increase of crime. Evenings one saw many drunken people, which was unusual. Gangs of men in surly mood made the streets unsafe, theft and assault were said to be frequent, even murder; for in two cases persons supposedly victims of the plague were proved to have been poisoned by their own families. And professional vice was rampant, displaying excesses heretofore unknown and only at home much farther south and in the east.

Such was the substance of the Englishman's tale. 'You would do well,' he concluded, 'to leave to-day instead of to-morrow. The blockade cannot be more than a few days off.'

'Thank you,' said Aschenbach, and left the office.

The Piazza lay in sweltering sunshine. Innocent foreigners sat before the cafés or stood in front of the cathedral, the centre of clouds of doves that, with fluttering wings, tried to shoulder each other away and pick the kernels of maize from the extended hand. Aschenbach strode up and down the spacious flags, feverishly excited, triumphant in possession of the truth at last, but with a sickening taste in his mouth and a fantastic horror at his heart. One decent, expiatory course lay open to him; he considered it. To-night, after dinner, he might approach the lady of the pearls and address her in words which he precisely formulated in his mind: 'Madame, will you permit an entire stranger to serve you with a word of advice and warning which self-interest prevents others from uttering? Go away. Leave here at once, without delay, with Tadzio and your daughters. Venice is in the grip of pestilence.' Then might he lay his hand in farewell upon the head of that instrument of a mocking deity; and thereafter himself flee the accursed morass. But he knew that he was far indeed from any serious desire to take such a step. It would restore him, would give him back himself once more; but he who is beside himself revolts at the idea of self-possession. There crossed his mind the vision of a white building with inscriptions on it, glittering in the sinking sun – he recalled how his mind had dreamed away into their transparent mysticism; recalled the strange pilgrim apparition that had wakened in the ageing man a lust for strange countries and fresh sights. And these memories again brought in their train the thought of return-ing home, returning to reason, self-mastery, an ordered existence, to the old life of effort. Alas! the bare thought made him wince with a revulsion that was like physical nausea. 'It must be kept quiet,' he whispered fiercely. 'I will not speak!' The knowledge that he shared the city's secret, the city's guilt – it put him beside himself, intoxicated him as a small quantity of wine will a man suffering from brain-fag. His thoughts dwelt upon the image of the desolate and calami-tous city, and he was giddy with fugitive, mad, unreasoning hopes and visions of a monstrous sweetness. That tender sentiment he had a moment ago evoked, what was it com-pared with such images as these? His art, his moral sense, what were they in the balance beside the boons that chaos might confer? He kept silence, he stopped on.

That night he had a fearful dream – if dream be the right word for a mental and physical experience which did indeed befall him in deep sleep, as a thing quite apart and real to his senses, yet without his seeing himself as present in it. Rather its theatre seemed to be his own soul, and the events burst in from outside, violently overcoming the profound resistance of his spirit; passed him through and left him, left the whole cultural structure of a life-time trampled on, ravaged, and destroyed.

The beginning was fear; fear and desire, with a shuddering curiosity. Night reigned, and his senses were on the alert; he heard loud, confused noises from far away, clamour and hubbub. There was a rattling, a crashing, a low dull thunder; shrill halloos and a kind of howl with a long-drawn *u*-sound at the end. And with all these, dominating them all, flute-notes of the cruellest sweetness, deep and cooing, keeping shamelessly on until the listener felt his very entrails bewitched. He heard a voice, naming, though darkly, that which was to come: 'The stranger god!' A glow lighted up the surrounding mist and by it he recognized a mountain scene like that about his country home. From the wooded heights, from among the tree-trunks and crumbling moss-covered rocks, a troop came tumbling and raging down, a whirling rout of men and animals, and overflowed the hillside with flames and human forms, with clamour and the reeling dance. The females stumbled over the long, hairy pelts that dangled from their girdles; with heads flung back they uttered loud hoarse cries and shook their tambourines high in air; brandished naked daggers or torches vomiting trails of sparks. They shrieked, holding their breasts in both hands; coiling snakes with quivering tongues they clutched about their waists. Horned and hairy males, girt about the loins with hides, drooped heads and lifted arms and thighs in unison, as they beat on brazen vessels that gave out droning thunder, or thumped madly on drums. There were troops of beardless youths armed with garlanded staves; these ran after goats and thrust their staves against the creatures' flanks, then clung to the plunging horns and let themselves be borne off with triumphant shouts. And one and all the mad rout yelled that cry, composed of soft consonants with a long-drawn *u*-sound at the end, so sweet and wild it was together, and like nothing ever heard before! It would ring through the air like the bellow of a challenging stag, and be given back many-tongued; or they would use it to goad each other on to dance with wild excess of tossing limbs – they never let it die. But the deep, beguiling notes of the flute wove in and out and over all. Beguiling too it was to him who struggled in the grip

of these sights and sounds, shamelessly awaiting the coming
feast and the uttermost surrender. He trembled, he shrank, his
will was steadfast to preserve and uphold his own god against
this stranger who was sworn enemy to dignity and self-control. But the mountain wall took up the noise and howling
and gave it back manifold; it rose high, swelled to a madness that carried him away. His senses reeled in the steam of
panting bodies, the acrid stench from the goats, the odour as
of stagnant waters – and another, too familiar smell – of
wounds, uncleanness, and disease. His heart throbbed to the
drums, his brain reeled, a blind rage seized him, a whirling
lust, he craved with all his soul to join the ring that formed
about the obscene symbol of the godhead, which they were
unveiling and elevating, monstrous and wooden, while from
full throats they yelled their rallying-cry. Foam dripped from
their lips, they drove each other on with lewd gesturings and
beckoning hands. They laughed, they howled, they thrust
their pointed staves into each other's flesh and licked the blood
as it ran down. But now the dreamer was in them and of them,
the stranger god was his own. Yes, it was he who was flinging
himself upon the animals, who bit and tore and swallowed
smoking gobbets of flesh – while on the trampled moss there
now began the rites in honour of the god, an orgy of promis-
cuous embraces – and in his very soul he tasted the bestial
degradation of his fall.

The unhappy man woke from this dream shattered, un-
hinged, powerless in the demon's grip. He no longer avoided
men's eyes nor cared whether he exposed himself to suspicion.
And anyhow, people were leaving; many of the bathing-
cabins stood empty, there were many vacant places in the
dining-room, scarcely any foreigners were seen in the streets.
The truth seemed to have leaked out; despite all efforts to the
contrary, panic was in the air. But the lady of the pearls
stopped on with her family; whether because the rumours
had not reached her or because she was too proud and fearless

to heed them. Tadzio remained; and it seemed at times to Aschenbach, in his obsessed state, that death and fear together might clear the island of all other souls and leave him there alone with him he coveted. In the long mornings on the beach his heavy gaze would rest, a fixed and reckless stare, upon the lad; towards nightfall, lost to shame, he would follow him through the city's narrow streets where horrid death stalked too, and at such time it seemed to him as though the moral law were fallen in ruins and only the monstrous and perverse held out a hope.

Like any lover, he desired to please; suffered agonies at the thought of failure, and brightened his dress with smart ties and handkerchiefs and other youthful touches. He added jewellery and perfumes and spent hours each day over his toilette, appearing at dinner elaborately arrayed and tensely excited. The presence of the youthful beauty that had bewitched him filled him with disgust of his own ageing body; the sight of his own sharp features and grey hair plunged him in hopeless mortification; he made desperate efforts to recover the appearance and freshness of his youth and began paying frequent visits to the hotel barber. Enveloped in the white sheet, beneath the hands of that garrulous personage, he would lean back in the chair and look at himself in the glass with misgiving.

'Grey,' he said, with a grimace.

'Slightly,' answered the man. 'Entirely due to neglect, to a lack of regard for appearances. Very natural, of course, in men of affairs, but, after all, not very sensible, for it is just such people who ought to be above vulgar prejudice in matters like these. Some folk have very strict ideas about the use of cosmetics; but they never extend them to the teeth, as they logically should. And very disgusted other people would be if they did. No, we are all as old as we feel, but no older, and grey hair can misrepresent a man worse than dyed. You, for instance, signore, have a right to your natural colour. Surely you will permit me to restore what belongs to you?'

'How?' asked Aschenbach.

For answer the oily one washed his client's hair in two waters, one clear and one dark, and lo, it was as black as in the days of his youth. He waved it with the tongs in wide, flat undulations, and stepped back to admire the effect.

'Now if we were just to freshen up the skin a little,' he said.

And with that he went on from one thing to another, his enthusiasm waxing with each new idea. Aschenbach sat there comfortably; he was incapable of objecting to the process – rather as it went forward it roused his hopes. He watched it in the mirror and saw his eyebrows grow more even and arching, the eyes gain in size and brilliance, by dint of a little application below the lids. A delicate carmine glowed on his cheeks where the skin had been so brown and leathery. The dry, anaemic lips grew full, they turned the colour of ripe strawberries, the lines round eyes and mouth were treated with a facial cream and gave place to youthful bloom. It was a young man who looked back at him from the glass – Aschenbach's heart leaped at the sight. The artist in cosmetic at last professed himself satisfied; after the manner of such people, he thanked his client profusely for what he had done himself. 'The merest trifle, the merest, signore,' he said as he added the final touches. 'Now the signore can fall in love as soon as he likes.' Aschenbach went off as in a dream, dazed between joy and fear, in his red neck-tie and broad straw hat with its gay striped band.

A lukewarm storm-wind had come up. It rained a little now and then, the air was heavy and turbid and smelt of decay. Aschenbach, with fevered cheeks beneath the rouge, seemed to hear rushing and flapping sounds in his ears, as though storm-spirits were abroad – unhallowed ocean harpies who follow those devoted to destruction, snatch away and defile their viands. For the heat took away his appetite and thus he was haunted with the idea that his food was infected.

One afternoon he pursued his charmer deep into the stricken

city's huddled heart. The labyrinthine little streets, squares, canals, and bridges, each one so like the next, at length quite made him lose his bearings. He did not even know the points of the compass; all his care was not to lose sight of the figure after which his eyes thirsted. He slunk under walls, he lurked behind buildings or people's backs; and the sustained tension of his senses and emotions exhausted him more and more, though for a long time he was unconscious of fatigue. Tadzio walked behind the others, he let them pass ahead in the narrow alleys, and as he sauntered slowly after, he would turn his head and assure himself with a glance of his strange, twilit grey eyes that his lover was still following. He saw him – and he did not betray him. The knowledge enraptured Aschenbach. Lured by those eyes, led on the leading-string of his own passion and folly, utterly lovesick, he stole upon the footsteps of his unseemly hope – and at the end found himself cheated. The Polish family crossed a small vaulted bridge, the height of whose archway hid them from his sight, and when he climbed it himself they were nowhere to be seen. He hunted in three directions – straight ahead and on both sides of the narrow, dirty quay – in vain. Worn quite out and un-nerved, he had to give over the search.

His head burned, his body was wet with clammy sweat, he was plagued by intolerable thirst. He looked about for refresh-ment, of whatever sort, and found a little fruit-shop where he bought some strawberries. They were overripe and soft; he ate them as he went. The street he was on opened out into a little square, one of those charmed, forsaken spots he liked; he recognized it as the very one where he had sat weeks ago and conceived his abortive plan of flight. He sank down on the steps of the well and leaned his head against its stone rim. It was quiet here. Grass grew between the stones and rubbish lay about. Tall, weather-beaten houses bordered the square, one of them rather palatial, with vaulted windows, gaping now, and little lion balconies. In the ground floor of another was an apothecary's shop. A waft of carbolic acid was borne on a warm gust of wind.

There he sat, the master: this was he who had found a way to reconcile art and honours; who had written *The Abject*, and in a style of classic purity renounced bohemianism and all its works, all sympathy with the abyss and the troubled depths of the outcast human soul. This was he who had put knowledge underfoot to climb so high; who had outgrown the ironic pose and adjusted himself to the burdens and obligations of fame; whose renown had been officially recognized and his name ennobled, whose style was set for a model in the schools. There he sat. His eyelids were closed, there was only a swift, sidelong glint of the eyeballs now and again, something between a question and a leer; while the rouged and flabby mouth uttered single words of the sentences shaped in his disordered brain by the fantastic logic that governs our dreams.

'For mark you, Phaedrus, beauty alone is both divine and visible; and so it is the sense's way, the artist's way, little Phaedrus, to the spirit. But, now tell me, my dear boy, do you believe that such a man can ever attain wisdom and true manly worth, for whom the path to the spirit must lead through the senses? Or do you rather think – for I leave the point to you – that it is a path of perilous sweetness, a way of transgression, and must surely lead him who walks in it astray? For you know that we poets cannot walk the way of beauty without Eros as our companion and guide. We may be heroic after our fashion, disciplined warriors of our craft, yet are we all like women, for we exult in passion, and love is still our desire – our craving and our shame. And from this you will perceive that we poets can be neither wise nor worthy citizens. We must needs be wanton, must needs rove at large in the realm of feeling. Our magisterial style is all folly and pretence, our honourable repute a farce, the crowd's belief in us is merely laughable. And to teach youth, or the populace, by means of art is a dangerous practice and ought to be forbidden. For what good can an artist be as a teacher, when from his birth up he is headed direct for the pit? We may want to shun it and attain to honour in the world; but however we turn, it draws us still. So, then, since knowledge might destroy us, we will have none of it. For knowledge, Phaedrus, does not make him who possesses it dignified or austere. Knowledge is all-knowing, understanding, forgiving; it takes up no position, sets no store by form. It has compassion with the abyss – it *is* the abyss. So we reject it, firmly, and henceforward our concern shall be with beauty only. And by beauty we mean simplicity, largeness, and renewed severity of discipline; we mean a return to detachment and to form. But detachment, Phaedrus, and preoccupation with form lead to intoxication and desire, they may lead the noblest among us to frightful emotional excesses, which his own stern cult of the beautiful would make him the first to condemn. So they too, they too, lead to the bottomless pit. Yes, they lead us thither, I say, us who are poets – who by our natures are prone not to excellence but to excess. And now, Phaedrus, I will go. Remain here; and only when you can no longer see me, then do you depart also.'

A few days later, Gustave Aschenbach left his hotel rather later than usual in the morning. He was not feeling well and had to struggle against spells of giddiness only half physical in their nature, accompanied by a swiftly mounting dread, a sense of futility and hopelessness – but whether this referred to himself or to the outer world he could not tell. In the lobby he saw a quantity of luggage lying strapped and ready; asked the porter whose it was, and received in answer the name he already knew he should hear – that of the Polish family. The expression of his ravaged features did not change; he only gave that quick lift of the head with which we sometimes receive the uninteresting answer to a casual query. But he put another: 'When?' 'After luncheon,' the man replied. He nodded, and went down to the beach.

It was an unfriendly scene. Little crisping shivers ran all across the wide stretch of shallow water between the shore and the first sand-bank. The whole beach, once so full of colour and life, looked now autumnal, out of season; it was nearly deserted and not even very clean. A camera on a tripod stood at the edge of the water, apparently abandoned; its black cloth snapped in the freshening wind.

Tadzio was there, in front of his cabin, with the three or four playfellows still left him. Aschenbach set up his chair some half-way between the cabins and the water, spread a rug over his knees, and sat looking on. The game this time was unsupervised, the elders being probably busy with the packing, and it looked rather lawless and out-of-hand. Jaschiu, the sturdy lad in the belted suit, with the black, brilliantined hair, became angry at a handful of sand thrown in his eyes; he challenged Tadzio to a fight, which quickly ended in the downfall of the weaker. And perhaps the coarser nature saw here a chance to avenge himself at last, by one cruel act, for his long weeks of subserviency: the victor would not let the vanquished get up, but remained kneeling on Tadzio's back, pressing Tadzio's face into the sand – for so long a time that it seemed the exhausted lad might even suffocate. He made spasmodic efforts to shake the other off, lay still and then began a feeble twitching. Just as Aschenbach was about to spring indignantly to the rescue, Jaschiu let his victim go. Tadzio, very pale, half sat up, and remained so, leaning on one arm, for several minutes, with darkening eyes and rumpled hair. Then he rose and walked slowly away. The others called him, at first gaily, then imploringly; he would not hear. Jaschiu was evidently overtaken by swift remorse; he followed his friend and tried to make his peace, but Tadzio motioned him back with a jerk of one shoulder and went down to the water's edge. He was barefoot and wore his striped linen suit with the red breast-knot.

There he stayed a little, with bent head, tracing figures in the wet sand with one toe; then stepped into the shallow water, which at its deepest did not wet his knees; waded idly through it and reached the sand-bar. Now he paused again with his face turned seaward; and next began to move slowly leftwards along the narrow strip of sand the sea left bare. He paced there, divided by an expanse of water from the shore, from his mates by his moody pride; a remote and isolated figure with floating locks, out there in sea and wind, against the misty inane. Once more he paused to look: with a sudden recollection, or by an impulse, he turned from the waist up, in an exquisite movement, one hand resting on his hip, and looked over his shoulder at the shore. The watcher sat just as he had sat that time in the lobby of the hotel when first the twilit grey eyes had met his own. He rested his head against the chair-back and followed the movements of the figure out there, then lifted it, as it were in answer to Tadzio's gaze. It sank on his breast, the eyes looked out beneath their lids, while his whole face took on the relaxed and brooding expression of deep slumber. It seemed to him the pale and lovely Summoner out there smiled at him and beckoned; as though with the hand he lifted from his hip, he pointed outward as he hovered on before into an immensity of richest expectation.

Some minutes passed before anyone hastened to the aid of the elderly man sitting there collapsed in his chair. They bore him to his room. And before nightfall a shocked and respectful world received the news of his decease.

1911

TRISTAN

*

EINFRIED, the sanatorium. A long, white, rectilinear building with a side wing, set in a spacious garden pleasingly equipped with grottoes, bowers, and little bark pavilions. Behind its slate roofs the mountains tower heavenwards, evergreen, massy, cleft with wooded ravines.

Now as then Dr Leander directs the establishment. He wears a two-pronged black beard as curly and wiry as horsehair stuffing; his spectacle-lenses are thick, and glitter; he has the look of a man whom science has cooled and hardened and filled with silent, forbearing pessimism. And with this beard, these lenses, this look, and in his short, reserved, preoccupied way, he holds his patients in his spell; holds those sufferers who, too weak to be laws unto themselves, put themselves into his hands that his severity may be a shield unto them.

As for Fräulein von Osterloh, hers it is to preside with unwearying zeal over the housekeeping. Ah, what activity! How she plies, now here, now there, now upstairs, now down, from one end of the building to the other! She is queen in kitchen and storerooms, she mounts the shelves of the linen-presses, she marshals the domestic staff; she ordains the bill of fare, to the end that the table shall be economical, hygienic, attractive, appetizing, and all these in the highest degree; she keeps house diligently, furiously; and her exceeding capacity conceals a constant reproach to the world of men, to no one of whom has it yet occurred to lead her to the altar. But ever on her cheeks there glows, in two round, carmine spots, the unquenchable hope of one day becoming Frau Dr Leander.

Ozone, and stirless, stirless air! Einfried, whatever Dr Leander's rivals and detractors may choose to say about it, can be most warmly recommended for lung patients. And not only these, but patients of all sorts, gentlemen, ladies, even children, come to stop here. Dr Leander's skill is challenged in many different fields. Sufferers from gastric disorders come, like Frau Magistrate Spatz – she has ear trouble into the bargain – people with defective hearts, paralytics, rheumatics, nervous sufferers of all kinds and degrees. A diabetic general here consumes his daily bread amid continual grumblings. There are several gentlemen with gaunt, fleshless faces who fling their legs about in that uncontrollable way that bodes no good. There is an elderly lady, a Frau Pastor Höhlenrauch, who has brought fourteen children into the world and is now incapable of a single thought, yet has not thereby attained to any peace of mind, but must go roving spectre-like all day long up and down through the house, on the arm of her private attendant, as she has been doing this year past.

Sometimes a death takes place among the 'severe cases', those who lie in their chambers, never appearing at meals or in the reception-rooms. When this happens no one knows of it, not even the person sleeping next door. In the silence of the night the waxen guest is put away and life at Einfried goes tranquilly on, with its massage, its electric treatment, douches, baths; with its exercises, its steaming and inhaling, in rooms especially equipped with all the triumphs of modern therapeutics.

Yes, a deal happens hereabouts – the institution is in a flourishing way. When new guests arrive, at the entrance to the side wing, the porter sounds the great gong; when there are departures, Dr Leander, together with Fräulein von Osterloh, conducts the traveller in due form to the waiting carriage. All sorts and kinds of people have received hospitality at Einfried. Even an author is here stealing time from God Almighty – a queer sort of man, with a name like some kind of mineral or precious stone.

Lastly there is, besides Dr Leander, another physician, who

takes care of the slight cases and the hopeless ones. But he bears the name of Müller and is not worth mentioning.

At the beginning of January a business man named Klöterjahn – of the firm of A. C. Klöterjahn & Co – brought his wife to Einfried. The porter rang the gong, and Fräulein von Osterloh received the guests from a distance in the drawing-room on the ground floor, which, like nearly all the fine old mansion, was furnished in wonderfully pure Empire style. Dr Leander appeared straightway. He made his best bow, and a preliminary conversation ensued, for the better information of both sides.

Beyond the windows lay the wintry garden, the flower-beds covered with straw, the grottoes snowed under, the little temples forlorn. Two porters were dragging in the guests' trunks from the carriage drawn up before the wrought-iron gate – for there was no drive up to the house.

'Be careful, Gabriele, *doucement, doucement*, my angel, keep your mouth closed,' Herr Klöterjahn had said as he led his wife through the garden; and nobody could look at her without tender-heartedly echoing the caution – though, to be sure, Herr Klöterjahn might quite as well have uttered it all in his own language.

The coachman who had driven the pair from the station to the sanatorium was an uncouth man, and insensitive; yet he sat with his tongue between his teeth as the husband lifted down his wife. The very horses, steaming in the frosty air, seemed to follow the procedure with their eyeballs rolled back in their heads out of sheer concern for so much tenderness and fragile charm.

The young wife's trouble was her trachea; it was expressly so set down in the letter Herr Klöterjahn had sent from the shores of the Baltic to announce their impending arrival to the director of Einfried – the trachea, and not the lungs, thank God! But it is a question whether, if it had been the lungs, the new patient could have looked any more pure and ethereal, any remoter from the concerns of this world, than she did now as she leaned back pale and weary in her chaste white-enamelled arm-chair, beside her robust husband, and listened to the conversation.

Her beautiful white hands, bare save for the simple wedding-ring, rested in her lap, among the folds of a dark, heavy cloth skirt; she wore a close-fitting waist of silver-grey with a stiff collar – it had an all-over pattern of arabesques in high-pile velvet. But these warm, heavy materials only served to bring out the unspeakable delicacy, sweetness, and languor of the little head, to make it look more than ever touching, exquisite and unearthly. Her light-brown hair was drawn smoothly back and gathered in a knot low in her neck, but near the right temple a single lock fell loose and curling, not far from the place where an odd little vein branched across one well-marked eyebrow, pale blue and sickly amid all that pure, well-nigh transparent spotlessness. That little blue vein above the eye dominated quite painfully the whole fine oval of the face. When she spoke, it stood out still more; yes, even when she smiled – and lent her expression a touch of strain, if not actually of distress, that stirred vague fear in the beholder. And yet she spoke, and she smiled: spoke frankly and pleasantly in her rather husky voice, with a smile in her eyes – though they again were sometimes a little difficult and showed a tendency to avoid a direct gaze. And the corners of her eyes, both sides of the base of the slender little nose, were deeply shadowed. She smiled with her mouth too, her beautiful wide mouth, whose lips were so pale and yet seemed to flash – perhaps because their contours were so exceedingly pure and well-cut. Sometimes she cleared her throat, then carried her handkerchief to her mouth and afterwards looked at it.

'Don't clear your throat like that, Gabriele,' said Herr Klöterjahn. 'You know, darling, Dr Hinzpeter expressly forbade it, and what we have to do is to exercise self-control, my angel. As I said, it is the trachea,' he repeated. 'Honestly, when it began, I thought it was the lungs, and it gave me a scare, I do assure you. But it isn't the lungs – we don't mean to let ourselves in for that, do we, Gabriele, my love, eh? Ha ha!'

'Surely not,' said Dr Leander, and glittered at her with his eye-glasses.

Whereupon Herr Klöterjahn ordered coffee, coffee and rolls; and the speaking way he had of sounding the *c* far back in his throat and exploding the *b* in 'butter' must have made any soul alive hungry to hear it.

His order was filled; and rooms were assigned to him and his wife, and they took possession with their things.

And Dr Leander took over the case himself, without calling in Dr Müller.

The population of Einfried took unusual interest in the fair new patient; Herr Klöterjahn, used as he was to see homage paid her, received it all with great satisfaction. The diabetic general, when he first saw her, stopped grumbling a minute; the gentlemen with the fleshless faces smiled and did their best to keep their legs in order; as for Frau Magistrate Spatz, she made her her oldest friend on the spot. Yes, she made an impression, this woman who bore Herr Klöterjahn's name! A writer who had been sojourning a few weeks in Einfried, a queer sort, he was, with a name like some precious stone or other, positively coloured up when she passed him in the corridor, stopped stock-still and stood there as though rooted to the ground, long after she had disappeared.

Before two days were out, the whole little population knew her history. She came originally from Bremen, as one could tell by certain pleasant small twists in her pronunciation; and it had been in Bremen that, two years gone by, she had bestowed her hand upon Herr Klöterjahn, a successful business man, and become his life-partner. She had followed him to his native town on the Baltic coast, where she had presented him, some ten months before the time of which we write, and under circumstances of the greatest difficulty and danger, with a child, a particularly well-formed and vigorous son and heir. But since that terrible hour she had never fully recovered her strength – granting, that is, that she had ever had any. She had not been long up, still extremely weak, with extremely impoverished vitality, when one day after coughing she brought up a little blood – oh, not much, an insignificant quantity in fact; but it would have been much better to be none at all; and the suspicious thing was, that the same trifling but disquieting incident recurred after another short while. Well, of course, there were things to be done, and Dr Hinzpeter, the family physician, did them. Complete rest was ordered, little pieces of ice swallowed; morphine administered to check the cough, and other medicines to regulate the heart action. But recovery failed to set in; and while the child, Anton Klöterjahn, junior, a magnificent specimen of a baby, seized on his place in life and held it with prodigious energy and ruthlessness, a low, unobservable fever seemed to waste the young mother daily. It was, as we have heard, an affection of the trachea – a word that in Dr Hinzpeter's mouth sounded so soothing, so consoling, so reassuring, that it raised their spirits to a surprising degree. But even though it was not the lungs, the doctor presently found that a milder climate and a stay in a sanatorium were imperative if the cure was to be hastened. The reputation enjoyed by Einfried and its director had done the rest.

Such was the state of affairs; Herr Klöterjahn himself related it to all and sundry. He talked with a slovenly pronunciation, in a loud, good-humoured voice, like a man whose digestion is in as capital order as his pocket-book; shovelling out the words pell-mell, in the broad accents of the northern coast-dweller; hurtling some of them forth so that each sound was a little explosion, at which he laughed as at a successful joke.

He was of medium height, broad, stout, and short-legged;

his face full and red, with watery blue eyes shaded by very fair lashes; with wide nostrils and humid lips. He wore English side-whiskers and English clothes, and it enchanted him to discover at Einfried an entire English family, father, mother and three pretty children with their nurse, who were stopping here for the simple and sufficient reason that they knew not where else to go. With this family he partook of a good English breakfast every morning. He set great store by good eating and drinking and proved to be a connoisseur both of food and wines, entertaining the other guests with the most exciting accounts of dinners given in his circle of acquaintance back home, with full descriptions of the choicer and rarer dishes; in the telling his eyes would narrow benignly, and his pronunciation take on certain palatal and nasal sounds, accompanied by smacking noises at the back of his throat. That he was not fundamentally averse to earthly joys of another sort was evinced upon an evening when a guest of the cure, an author by calling, saw him in the corridor trifling in not quite permissible fashion with a chambermaid – a humorous little passage at which the author in question made a laughably disgusted face.

As for Herr Klöterjahn's wife, it was plain to see that she was devotedly attached to her husband. She followed his words and movements with a smile: not the rather arrogant toleration the ailing sometimes bestow upon the well and sound, but the sympathetic participation of a well-disposed invalid in the manifestations of people who rejoice in the blessing of abounding health.

Herr Klöterjahn did not stop long in Einfried. He had brought his wife hither, but when a week had gone by and he knew she was in good hands and well looked after, he did not linger. Duties equally weighty – his flourishing child, his no less flourishing business – took him away; they compelled him to go, leaving her rejoicing in the best of care.

Spinell was the name of that author who had been stopping

some weeks in Einfried – Detlev Spinell was his name, and
his looks were quite out of the common. Imagine a dark man
at the beginning of the thirties, impressively tall, with hair
already distinctly grey at the temples, and a round, white,
slightly bloated face, without a vestige of beard. Not that it
was shaven – that you could have told; it was soft, smooth,
boyish, with at most a downy hair here and there. And the
effect was singular. His bright, doe-like brown eyes had a
gentle expression, the nose was thick and rather too fleshy.
Also, Herr Spinell had an upper lip like an ancient Roman's,
swelling and full of pores; large, carious teeth, and feet of uncommon size. One of the gentlemen with the rebellious legs,
a cynic and ribald wit, had christened him 'the dissipated
baby'; but the epithet was malicious, and not very apt. Herr
Spinell dressed well, in a long black coat and a waistcoat with
coloured spots.

He was unsocial and sought no man's company. Only once
in a while he might be overtaken by an affable, blithe, expan-
sive mood; and this always happened when he was carried
away by an aesthetic fit at the sight of beauty, the harmony of
two colours, a vase nobly formed, or the range of mountains
lighted by the setting sun. 'How beautiful!' he would say,
with his head on one side, his shoulders raised, his hands
spread out, his lips and nostrils curled and distended. 'My God!
look, how beautiful!' And in such moments of ardour he was
quite capable of flinging his arms blindly round the neck of anybody, high or low, male or female, that happened to be near.

On his table, for anybody to see who entered his room,
there always lay the book he had written. It was a novel of
medium length, with a perfectly bewildering drawing on the
jacket, printed on a sort of filter-paper. Each letter of the type
looked like a Gothic cathedral. Fräulein von Osterloh had
read it once, in a spare quarter-hour, and found it 'very cultured' – which was her circumlocution for inhumanly bore-
some. Its scenes were laid in fashionable salons, in luxurious

boudoirs full of choice *objets d'art*, old furniture, gobelins, rare porcelains, priceless stuffs, and art treasures of all sorts and kinds. On the description of these things was expended the most loving care; as you read you constantly saw Herr Spinell, with distended nostrils, saying: 'How beautiful! My God! look, how beautiful!' After all, it was strange he had not written more than this one book; he so obviously adored writing. He spent the greater part of the day doing it, in his room, and sent an extraordinary number of letters to the post, two or three nearly every day – and that made it more striking, even almost funny, that he very seldom received one in return.

Herr Spinell sat opposite Herr Klöterjahn's wife. At the first meal of which the new guests partook, he came rather late into the dining-room, on the ground floor of the side wing, bade good-day to the company generally in a soft voice, and betook himself to his own place, whereupon Dr Leander perfunctorily presented him to the new-comers. He bowed, and self-consciously began to eat, using his knife and fork rather affectedly with the large, finely shaped white hands that came out from his very narrow coat-sleeves. After a little he grew more at ease and looked tranquilly first at Herr Klöterjahn and then at his wife, by turns. And in the course of the meal Herr Klöterjahn addressed to him sundry queries touching the general situation and climate of Einfried; his wife, in her charming way, added a word or two, and Herr Spinell gave courteous answers. His voice was mild, and really agreeable; but he had a halting way of speaking that almost amounted to an impediment – as though his teeth got in the way of his tongue.

After luncheon, when they had gone into the salon, Dr Leander came up to the new arrivals to wish them *Mahlzeit*, and Herr Klöterjahn's wife took occasion to ask about their *vis-à-vis*.

'What was the gentleman's name?' she asked. 'I did not quite catch it. Spinelli?'

'Spinell, not Spinelli, madame. No, he is not an Italian; he only comes from Lemberg, I believe.'

'And what was it you said? He is an author, or something of the sort?' asked Herr Klöterjahn. He had his hands in the pockets of his very easy-fitting English trousers, cocked his head towards the doctor, and opened his mouth, as some people do, to listen the better.

'Yes . . . I really don't know,' answered Dr Leander. 'He writes. . . . I believe he has written a book, some sort of novel. I really don't know what.'

By which Dr Leander conveyed that he had no great opinion of the author and declined all responsibility on the score of him.

'But I find that most interesting,' said Herr Klöterjahn's wife. Never before had she met an author face to face.

'Oh, yes,' said Dr Leander obligingly. 'I understand he has a certain amount of reputation,' which closed the conversation.

But a little later, when the new guests had retired and Dr Leander himself was about to go, Herr Spinell detained him in talk to put a few questions for his own part.

'What was their name?' he asked. 'I did not understand a syllable, of course.'

'Klöterjahn,' answered Dr Leander, turning away.

'What's that?' asked Herr Spinell.

'*Klöterjahn* is their name,' said Dr Leander, and went his way. He set no great store by the author.

Have we got as far on as where Herr Klöterjahn went home? Yes, he was back on the shore of the Baltic once more, with his business and his babe, that ruthless and vigorous little being who had cost his mother great suffering and a slight weakness of the trachea; while she herself, the young wife, remained in Einfried and became the intimate friend of Frau Spatz. Which did not prevent Herr Klöterjahn's wife from being on friendly

terms with the rest of the guests – for instance with Herr
Spinell, who, to the astonishment of everybody, for he had
up to now held communion with not a single soul, displayed
from the very first an extraordinary devotion and courtesy,
and with whom she enjoyed talking, whenever she had any
time left over from the stern service of the cure.

He approached her with immense circumspection and reverence, and never spoke save with his voice so carefully subdued that Frau Spatz, with her bad hearing, seldom or never
caught anything he said. He tiptoed on his great feet up to the
arm-chair in which Herr Klöterjahn's wife leaned, fragilely
smiling; stopped two paces off, with his body bent forward
and one leg poised behind him, and talked in his halting way,
as though he had an impediment in his speech; with ardour,
yet prepared to retire at any moment and vanish at the first
sign of fatigue or satiety. But he did not tire her; she begged
him to sit down with her and the Rätin; she asked him questions and listened with curious smiles, for he had a way of
talking sometimes that was so odd and amusing, different
from anything she had ever heard before.

'Why are you in Einfried, really?' she asked. 'What cure
are you taking, Herr Spinell?'

'Cure? Oh, I'm having myself electrified a bit. Nothing
worth mentioning. I will tell you the real reason why I am
here, madame. It is a feeling for style.'

'Ah?' said Herr Klöterjahn's wife; supported her chin on
her hand and turned to him with exaggerated eagerness, as
one does to a child who wants to tell a story.

'Yes, madame. Einfried is perfect Empire. It was once a
castle, a summer residence, I am told. This side wing is a later
addition, but the main building is old and genuine. There are
times when I cannot endure Empire, and then times when I
simply must have it in order to attain any sense of well-being.
Obviously, people feel one way among furniture that is soft
and comfortable and voluptuous, and quite another among

the straight lines of these tables, chairs and draperies. This brightness and hardness, this cold, austere simplicity and reserved strength, madame – it has upon me the ultimate effect of an inward purification and rebirth. Beyond a doubt, it is morally elevating.'

'Yes, that is remarkable,' she said. 'And when I try I can understand what you mean.'

Whereto he responded that it was not worth her taking any sort of trouble, and they laughed together. Frau Spatz laughed too and found it remarkable in her turn, though she did not say she understood it.

The reception-room was spacious and beautiful. The high white folding doors that led to the billiard-room were wide open, and the gentlemen with the rebellious legs were disporting themselves within, others as well. On the opposite side of the room a glass door gave on the broad veranda and the garden. Near the door stood a piano. At a green-covered folding table, the diabetic general was playing whist with some other gentlemen. Ladies sat reading or embroidering. The rooms were heated by an iron stove, but the chimney-piece, in the purest style, had coals pasted over with red paper to simulate a fire, and chairs were drawn up invitingly.

'You are an early riser, Herr Spinell,' said Herr Klöterjahn's wife. 'Two or three times already I have chanced to see you leaving the house at half past seven in the morning.'

'An early riser? Ah, with a difference, madame, with a vast difference. The truth is, I rise early because I am such a late sleeper.'

'You really must explain yourself, Herr Spinell.' Frau Spatz too said she demanded an explanation.

'Well, if one is an early riser, one does not need to get up so early. Or so it seems to me. The conscience, madame, is a bad business. I, and other people like me, work hard all our lives to swindle our consciences into feeling pleased and satisfied. We are feckless creatures, and aside from a few good hours

we go around weighted down, sick and sore with the knowledge of our own futility. We hate the useful; we know it is
vulgar and unlovely, and we defend this position, as a man
defends something that is absolutely necessary to his existence.
Yet all the while conscience is gnawing at us, to such an
extent that we are simply one wound. Added to that, our
whole inner life, our view of the world, our way of working,
is of a kind – its effect is frightfully unhealthy, undermining,
irritating, and this only aggravates the situation. Well, then,
there are certain little counter-irritants, without which we
would most certainly not hold out. A kind of decorum, a
hygienic regimen, for instance, becomes a necessity for some
of us. To get up early, to get up ghastly early, take a cold
bath, and go out walking in a snowstorm – that may give us
a sense of self-satisfaction that lasts as much as an hour. If I
were to act out my true character, I should be lying in bed
late into the afternoon. My getting up early is all hypocrisy,
believe me.'

'Why do you say that, Herr Spinell? On the contrary, I
call it self-abnegation.' Frau Spatz, too, called it self-abnegation.

'Hypocrisy or self-abnegation – call it what you like,
madame. I have such a hideously downright nature – –'

'Yes, that's it. Surely you torment yourself far too much.'

'Yes, madame, I torment myself a great deal.'

The fine weather continued. Rigid and spotless white the
region lay, the mountains, house and garden, in a windless air
that was blinding clear and cast bluish shadows; and above it
arched the spotless pale-blue sky, where myriads of bright
particles of glittering crystals seemed to dance. Herr Klöterjahn's wife felt tolerably well these days: free of fever, with
scarce any cough, and able to eat without too great distaste.
Many days she sat taking her cure for hours on end in the
sunny cold on the terrace. She sat in the snow, bundled in
wraps and furs, and hopefully breathed in the pure icy air to

do her trachea good. Sometimes she saw Herr Spinell, dressed like herself, and in fur boots that made his feet a fantastic size, taking an airing in the garden. He walked with tentative tread through the snow, holding his arms in a certain careful pose that was stiff yet not without grace; coming up to the terrace he would bow very respectfully and mount the first step or so to exchange a few words with her.

'To-day on my morning walk I saw a beautiful woman – good Lord! how beautiful she was!' he said; laid his head on one side and spread out his hands.

'Really, Herr Spinell. Do describe her to me.'

'That I cannot do. Or, rather, it would not be a fair picture. I only saw the lady as I glanced at her in passing. I did not actually see her at all. But that fleeting glimpse was enough to rouse my fancy and make me carry away a picture so beautiful that – good Lord! how beautiful it is!'

She laughed. 'Is that the way you always look at beautiful women, Herr Spinell? Just a fleeting glance?'

'Yes, madame; it is a better way than if I were avid of actuality, stared them plump in the face, and carried away with me only a consciousness of the blemishes they in fact possess.'

'"Avid of actuality" – what a strange phrase, a regular literary phrase, Herr Spinell; no one but an author could have said that. It impresses me very much, I must say. There is a lot in it that I dimly understand; there is something free about it, and independent, that even seems to be looking down on reality though it is so very respectable – is respectability itself, as you might say. And it makes me comprehend, too, that there is something else besides the tangible, something more subtle – –'

'I know only one face,' he said suddenly, with a strange lift in his voice, carrying his closed hands to his shoulders as he spoke and showing his carious teeth in an almost hysterical smile. 'I know only one face of such lofty nobility that the mere thought of enhancing it through my imagination would be blasphemous; at which I could wish to look, on which I could wish to dwell, not minutes and not hours, but my whole life long; losing myself utterly therein, forgotten to every earthly thought. . . .'

'Yes, indeed, Herr Spinell. And yet don't you find Fräulein von Osterloh has rather prominent ears?'

He replied only by a profound bow; then, standing erect, let his eyes rest with a look of embarrassment and pain on the strange little vein that branched pale-blue and sickly across her pure translucent brow.

An odd sort, a very odd sort. Herr Klöterjahn's wife thought about him sometimes; for she had much leisure for thought. Whether it was that the change of air began to lose its effect or some positively detrimental influence was at work, she began to go backward, the condition of her trachea left much to be desired, she had fever not infrequently, felt tired and exhausted, and could not eat. Dr Leander most emphatically recommended rest, quiet, caution, care. So she sat, when indeed she was not forced to lie, quite motionless, in the society of Frau Spatz, holding some sort of sewing which she did not sew, and following one or another train of thought.

Yes, he gave her food for thought, this very odd Herr Spinell; and the strange thing was she thought not so much about him as about herself, for he had managed to rouse in her a quite novel interest in her own personality. One day he had said, in the course of conversation:

'No, they are positively the most enigmatic facts in nature – women, I mean. That is a truism, and yet one never ceases to marvel at it afresh. Take some wonderful creature, a sylph, an airy wraith, a fairy dream of a thing, and what does she do? Goes and gives herself to a brawny Hercules at a country fair, or maybe to a butcher's apprentice. Walks about on his arm, even leans her head on his shoulder and looks round with an impish smile as if to say: "Look on this, if you like, and break you heads over it." And we break them.'

With this speech Herr Klöterjahn's wife had occupied her leisure again and again.

Another day, to the wonderment of Frau Spatz, the following conversation took place:

'May I ask, madame – though you may very likely think me prying – what your name really is?'

'Why, Herr Spinell, you know my name is Klöterjahn!'

'H'm. Yes, I know that – or, rather, I deny it. I mean your own name, your maiden name, of course. You will in justice, madame, admit that anybody who calls you Klöterjahn ought to be thrashed.'

She laughed so hard that the little blue vein stood out alarmingly on her brow and gave the pale sweet face a strained expression disquieting to see.

'Oh, no! Not at all, Herr Spinell! Thrashed, indeed! Is the name Klöterjahn so horrible to you?'

'Yes, madame. I hate the name from the bottom of my heart. I hated it the first time I heard it. It is the abandonment of ugliness; it is grotesque to make you comply with the custom so far as to fasten your husband's name upon you; it is barbarous and vile.'

'Well, and how about Eckhof? Is that any better? Eckhof is my father's name.'

'Ah, you see! Eckhof is quite another thing. There was a great actor named Eckhof. Eckhof will do nicely. You spoke of your father – Then is your mother – –?'

'Yes, my mother died when I was little.'

'Ah! Tell me a little more of yourself, pray. But not if it tires you. When it tires you, stop, and I will go on talking about Paris, as I did the other day. But you could speak very softly, or even whisper – that would be more beautiful still. You were born in Bremen?' He breathed, rather than uttered, the question with an expression so awed, so heavy with import, as to suggest that Bremen was a city like no other on earth, full of hidden beauties and nameless adventures, and ennobling in some mysterious way those born within its walls.

'Yes, imagine,' said she involuntarily. 'I was born in Bremen.'

'I was there once,' he thoughtfully remarked.

'Goodness me, you have been there, too? Why, Herr Spinell, it seems to me you must have been everywhere there is between Spitsbergen and Tunis!'

'Yes, I was there once,' he repeated. 'A few hours, one evening. I recall a narrow old street, with a strange, warped-looking moon above the gabled roofs. Then I was in a cellar that smelled of wine and mould. It is a poignant memory.'

'Really? Where could that have been, I wonder? Yes, in just such a grey old gabled house I was born, one of the old merchant houses, with echoing wooden floor and white-painted gallery.'

'Then your father is a business man?' he asked hesitatingly.

'Yes, but he is also, and in the first place, an artist.'

'Ah! In what way?'

'He plays the violin. But just saying that does not mean much. It is *how* he plays, Herr Spinell – it is that that matters! Sometimes I cannot listen to some of the notes without the tears coming into my eyes and making them burn. Nothing else in the world makes me feel like that. You won't believe it – –'

'But I do. Oh, very much I believe it! Tell me, madame, your family is old, is it not? Your family has been living for generations in the old gabled house – living and working and closing their eyes on time? – '

'Yes. Tell me why you ask.'

'Because it not infrequently happens that a race with sober, practical bourgeois traditions will towards the end of its days flare up in some form of art.'

'Is that a fact?'

'Yes.'

'It is true, my father is surely more of an artist than some that call themselves so and get the glory of it. I only play the piano a little. They have forbidden me now, but at home, in the old days, I still played. Father and I played together. Yes, I have precious memories of all those years; and especially of the garden, our garden, behind the house. It was dreadfully wild and overgrown, and shut in by crumbling mossy walls. But it was just that that gave it such charm. In the middle was a fountain with a wide border of sword-lilies. In summer I spent long hours there with my friends. We all sat round the fountain on little camp-stools – –'

'How beautiful!' said Herr Spinell, and flung up his shoulders. 'You sat there and sang?'

'No, we mostly crocheted.'

'But still – –'

'Yes, we crocheted and chattered, my six friends and I – –'

'How beautiful! Good Lord! think of it, *how beautiful!*' cried Herr Spinell again, his face quite distorted with emotion.

'Now, what is it you find so particularly beautiful about that, Herr Spinell?'

'Oh, there being six of them besides you, and your being not one of the six, but a queen among them . . . set apart from your six friends. A little gold crown showed in your hair – quite a modest, unostentatious little crown, still it was there – –'

'Nonsense, there was nothing of the sort.'

'Yes, there was; it shone unseen. But if I had been there, standing among the shrubbery, one of those times I should have seen it.'

'God knows what you would have seen. But you were not there. Instead of that, it was my husband who came out of the shrubbery one day, with my father. I was afraid they had been listening to our prattle – –'

'So it was there, then, madame, that you first met your husband?'

'Yes, there it was I saw him first,' she said, in quite a glad, strong voice; she smiled, and as she did so the little blue vein came out and gave her face a constrained and anxious expression. 'He was calling on my father on business, you see. Next day he came to dinner, and three days later he proposed for my hand.'

'Really? It all happened as fast as that?'

'Yes. Or, rather, it went a little slower after that. For my father was not very much inclined to it, you see, and consented on condition that we wait a long time first. He would rather I had stopped with him, and he had doubts in other ways too. But – –'

'But?'

'But I had set my heart on it,' she said, smiling; and once more the little vein dominated her whole face with its look of constraint and anxiety.

'Ah, so you set your heart on it.'

'Yes, and I displayed great strength of purpose, as you see – –'

'As I see. Yes.'

'So that my father had to give way in the end.'

'And so you forsook him and his fiddle and the old house with the overgrown garden, and the fountain and your six friends, and clave unto Herr Klöterjahn – –'

' "And clave unto" – you have such a strange way of saying things, Herr Spinell. Positively biblical. Yes, I forsook all that; nature has arranged things that way.'

'Yes, I suppose that is it.'

'And it was a question of my happiness – –'

'Of course. And happiness came to you?'

'It came, Herr Spinell, in the moment when they brought little Anton to me, our little Anton, and he screamed so lustily with his strong little lungs – he is very, very strong and healthy, you know – –'

'This is not the first time, madame, that I have heard you

speak of your little Anton's good health and great strength. He must be quite uncommonly healthy?'

'That he is. And looks so absurdly like my husband!'

'Ah! . . . So that was the way of it. And now you are no longer called by the name of Eckhof, but a different one, and you have your healthy little Anton, and are troubled with your trachea.'

'Yes. And you are a perfectly enigmatic man, Herr Spinell, I do assure you.'

'Yes, God knows you certainly are,' said Frau Spatz, who was present on this occasion.

And that conversation, too, gave Herr Klöterjahn's wife food for reflection. Idle as it was, it contained much to nourish those secret thoughts of hers about herself. Was this the baleful influence which was at work? Her weakness increased and fever often supervened, a quiet glow in which she rested with a feeling of mild elevation, to which she yielded in a pensive mood that was a little affected, self-satisfied, even rather self-righteous. When she had not to keep her bed, Herr Spinell would approach her with immense caution, tiptoeing on his great feet; he would pause two paces off, with his body inclined and one leg behind him, and speak in a voice that was hushed with awe, as though he would lift her higher and higher on the tide of his devotion until she rested on billowy cushions of cloud where no shrill sound nor any earthly touch might reach her. And when he did this she would think of the way Herr Klöterjahn said: 'Take care, my angel, keep your mouth closed, Gabriele,' a way that made her feel as though he had struck her roughly though well-meaningly on the shoulder. Then as fast as she could she would put the memory away and rest in her weakness and elevation of spirit upon the clouds which Herr Spinell spread out for her.

One day she abruptly returned to the talk they had had about her early life. 'Is it really true, Herr Spinell,' she asked, 'that you would have seen the little gold crown?'

Two weeks had passed since that conversation, yet he knew at once what she meant, and his voice shook as he assured her that he would have seen the little crown as she sat among her friends by the fountain – would have caught its fugitive gleam among her locks.

A few days later one of the guests chanced to make a polite inquiry after the health of little Anton. Herr Klöterjahn's wife gave a quick glance at Herr Spinell, who was standing near, and answered in a perfunctory voice:

'Thanks, how should he be? He and my husband are quite well, of course.'

There came a day at the end of February, colder, purer, more brilliant than any that had come before it, and high spirits held sway at Einfried. The 'heart cases' consulted in groups, flushed of cheek, the diabetic general carolled like a boy out of school, and the gentlemen of the rebellious legs cast aside all restraint. And the reason for all these things was that a sleighing party was in prospect, an excursion in sledges into the mountains, with cracking whips and sleigh-bells jingling. Dr Leander had arranged this diversion for his patients.

The serious cases, of course, had to stop at home. Poor things! The other guests arranged to keep it from them; it did them good to practise this much sympathy and consideration. But a few of those remained at home who might very well have gone. Fräulein von Osterloh was of course excused, she had too much on her mind to permit her even to think of going. She was needed at home, and at home she remained. But the disappointment was general when Herr Klöterjahn's wife announced her intention of stopping away. Dr Leander exhorted her to come and get the benefit of the fresh air – but in vain. She said she was not up to it, she had a headache, she felt too weak – they had to resign themselves. The cynical gentleman took occasion to say:

'You will see, the dissipated baby will stop at home too.'

And he proved to be right, for Herr Spinnell gave out that he intended to 'work' that afternoon – he was prone thus to characterize his dubious activities. Anyhow, not a soul regretted his absence; nor did they take more to heart the news that Frau Magistrate Spatz had decided to keep her young friend company at home – sleighing made her feel sea-sick.

Luncheon on the great day was eaten as early as twelve o'clock, and immediately thereafter the sledges drew up in front of Einfried. The guests came through the garden in little groups, warmly wrapped, excited, full of eager anticipation. Herr Klöterjahn's wife stood with Frau Spatz at the glass door which gave on the terrace, while Herr Spinell watched the setting-forth from above, at the window of his room. They saw the little struggles that took place for the best seats, amid joking and laughter; Fräulein von Osterloh, with a fur boa round her neck, running from one sleigh to the other and shoving baskets of provisions under the seats; they saw Dr Leander, with his fur cap pulled low on his brow, marshalling the whole scene with his spectacle-lenses glittering, to make sure everything was ready. At last he took his own seat and gave the signal to drive off. The horses started up, a few of the ladies shrieked and collapsed, the bells jingled, the short-shafted whips cracked and their long lashes trailed across the snow; Fräulein von Osterloh stood at the gate waving her handkerchief until the train rounded a curve and disappeared; slowly the merry tinkling died away. Then she turned and hastened back through the garden in pursuit of her duties; the two ladies left the glass door, and almost at the same time Herr Spinell abandoned his post of observation above.

Quiet reigned at Einfried. The party would not return before evening. The serious cases lay in their rooms and suffered. Herr Klöterjahn's wife took a short turn with her friend, then they went to their respective chambers. Herr

Spinell kept to his, occupied in his own way. Towards four o'clock the ladies were served with half a litre of milk apiece, and Herr Spinell with a light tea. Soon after, Herr Klöterjahn's wife tapped on the wall between her room and Frau Spatz's and called:

'Shan't we go down to the salon, Frau Spatz? I have nothing to do up here.'

'In just a minute, my dear,' answered she. 'I'll just put on my shoes – if you will wait a minute. I have been lying down.'

The salon, naturally, was empty. The ladies took seats by the fireplace. The Frau Magistrate embroidered flowers on a strip of canvas; Herr Klöterjahn's wife took a few stitches too, but soon let her work fall in her lap and, leaning on the arm of her chair, fell to dreaming. At length she made some remark hardly worth the trouble of opening her lips for; the Frau Magistrate asked what she said, and she had to make the effort of saying it all over again, which quite wore her out. But just then steps were heard outside, the door opened, and Herr Spinell came in.

'Shall I be disturbing you?' he asked mildly from the threshold, addressing Herr Klöterjahn's wife and her alone; bending over her, as it were, from a distance, in the tender, hovering way he had.

The young wife answered:

'Why should you? The room is free to everybody – and besides, why would it be disturbing us? On the contrary, I am convinced that I am boring Frau Spatz.'

He had no ready answer, merely smiled and showed his carious teeth, then went hesitatingly up to the glass door, the ladies watching him, and stood with his back to them looking out. Presently he half turned round, still gazing into the garden, and said:

'The sun has gone in. The sky clouded over without our seeing it. The dark is coming on already.'

'Yes, it is all overcast,' replied Herr Klöterjahn's wife. 'It looks as though our sleighing party would have some snow after all. Yesterday at this hour it was still broad daylight, now it is already getting dark.'

'Well,' he said, 'after all these brilliant weeks a little dullness is good for the eyes. The sun shines with the same penetrating clearness upon the lovely and the commonplace, and I for one am positively grateful to it for finally going under a cloud.'

'Don't you like the sun, Herr Spinell?'

'Well, I am no painter . . . when there is no sun one becomes more profound. . . . It is a thick layer of greyish-white cloud. Perhaps it means thawing weather for to-morrow. But, madame, let me advise you not to sit there at the back of the room looking at your embroidery.'

'Don't be alarmed; I am not looking at it. But what else is there to do?'

He had sat down on the piano-stool, resting one arm on the lid of the instrument.

'Music,' he said. 'If we could only have a little music here. The English children sing darky songs, and that is all.'

'And yesterday afternoon Fräulein von Osterloh rendered "Cloister Bells" at top speed,' remarked Herr Klöterjahn's wife.

'But you play, madame!' said he, in an imploring tone. He stood up. 'Once you used to play every day with your father.'

'Yes, Herr Spinell, in those old days I did. In the time of the fountain, you know.'

'Play to us to-day,' he begged. 'Just a few notes – this once. If you knew how I long for some music – –'

'But our family physician, as well as Dr Leander, expressly forbade it, Herr Spinell.'

'But they aren't here – either of them. We are free agents. Just a few bars – –'

'No, Herr Spinell, it would be no use. Goodness knows what marvels you expect of me – and I have forgotten everything I knew. Truly. I know scarcely anything by heart.'

'Well, then, play that scarcely anything. But there are notes here too. On top of the piano. No, that is nothing. But there is some Chopin.'

'Chopin?'

'Yes, the Nocturnes. All we have to do is to light the candles – –'

'Pray don't ask me to play, Herr Spinell. I must not. Suppose it were to be bad for me – –'

He was silent; standing there in the light of the two candles, with his great feet, in his long black tail-coat, with his beardless face and greying hair. His hands hung down at his sides. 'Then, madame, I will ask no more,' he said at length, in a low voice. 'If you are afraid it will do you harm, then we shall leave the beauty dead and dumb that might have come alive beneath your fingers. You were not always so sensible; at least not when it was the opposite question from what it is to-day, and you had to decide to take leave of beauty. Then you did not care about your bodily welfare; you showed a firm and unhesitating resolution when you left the fountain and laid aside the little gold crown. Listen,' he said, after a pause, and his voice dropped still lower; 'if you sit down and play as you used to play when your father stood behind you and brought tears to your eyes with the tones of his violin – who knows but the little gold crown might glimmer once more in your hair. . . .'

'Really,' said she, with a smile. Her voice happened to break on the word, it sounded husky and barely audible. She cleared her throat and went on:

'Are those really Chopin's Nocturnes you have there?'

'Yes, here they are open at the place; everything is ready.'

'Well, then, in God's name, I will play one,' said she. 'But only one – do you hear? In any case, one will do you, I am sure.'

With which she got up, laid aside her work, and went to the piano. She seated herself on the music-stool, on a few bound volumes, arranged the lights and turned over the notes. Herr Spinell had drawn up a chair and sat beside her, like a music-master.

She played the Nocturne in E major, opus 9, number 2. If her playing had really lost very much then she must originally have been a consummate artist. The piano was mediocre, but after the first few notes she learned to control it. She displayed a nervous feeling for modulations of timbre and a joy in mobility of rhythm that amounted to the fantastic. Her attack was at once firm and soft. Under her hands the very last drop of sweetness was wrung from the melody; the embellishments seemed to cling with slow grace about her limbs.

She wore the same frock as on the day of her arrival, the dark, heavy bodice with the velvet arabesques in high relief, that gave her head and hands such an unearthly fragile look. Her face did not change as she played but her lips seemed to become more clear-cut, the shadows deepened at the corners of her eyes. When she finished she laid her hands in her lap and went on looking at the notes. Herr Spinell sat motionless.

She played another Nocturne, and then a third. Then she stood up, but only to look on the top of the piano for more music.

It occurred to Herr Spinell to look at the black-bound volumes on the piano-stool. All at once he uttered an incoherent exclamation, his large white hands clutching at one of the books.

'Impossible! No, it cannot be,' he said. 'But yes, it is. Guess what this is – what was lying here! Guess what I have in my hands.'

'What?' she asked.

Mutely he showed her the title-page. He was quite pale; he let the book sink and looked at her, his lips trembling.

'Really? How did that get here? Give it me,' was all she said; set the notes on the piano and after a moment's silence began to play.

He sat beside her, bent forward, his hands between his knees, his head bowed. She played the beginning with exaggerated and tormenting slowness, with painfully long pauses between the single figures. The *Sehnsuchtsmotiv*, roving lost and forlorn like a voice in the night, lifted its trembling question. Then silence, a waiting. And lo, an answer: the same timorous, lonely note, only clearer, only tenderer. Silence again. And then, with that marvellous muted *sforzando*, like mounting passion, the love-motif came in; reared and soared and yearned ecstatically upward to its consummation, sank back, was resolved; the cellos taking up the melody to carry it on with their deep, heavy notes of rapture and despair.

Not unsuccessfully did the player seek to suggest the orchestral effects upon the poor instrument at her command. The violin runs of the great climax rang out with brilliant precision. She played with a fastidious reverence, lingering on each figure, bringing out each detail, with the self-forgotten concentration of the priest who lifts the Host above his head. Here two forces, two beings, strove towards each other, in transports of joy and pain; here they embraced and became one in delirious yearning after eternity and the absolute. . . . The prelude flamed up and died away. She stopped at the point where the curtains part, and sat speechless, staring at the keys.

But the boredom of Frau Spatz had by now reached that pitch where it distorts the countenance of man, makes the eyes protrude from the head, and lends the features a corpse-like and terrifying aspect. More than that, this music acted on the nerves that controlled her digestion, producing in her dyspeptic organism such *malaise* that she was really afraid she would have an attack.

'I shall have to go up to my room,' she said weakly. 'Good-bye; I will come back soon.'

She went out. Twilight was far advanced. Outside the snow fell thick and soundlessly upon the terrace. The two tapers cast a flickering, circumscribed light.

'The Second Act,' he whispered, and she turned the pages and began.

What was it dying away in the distance – the ring of a horn? The rustle of leaves? The rippling of a brook? Silence and night crept up over grove and house; the power of longing had full sway, no prayers or warnings could avail against it. The holy mystery was consummated. The light was quenched, with a strange clouding of the timbre the death-motif sank down: white-veiled desire, by passion driven, fluttered towards love as through the dark it groped to meet her.

Ah, boundless, unquenchable exultation of union in the eternal beyond! Freed from torturing error, escaped from fettering space and time, the Thou and the I, the Thine and the Mine at one forever in a sublimity of bliss! The day might part them with deluding show; but when night fell, then by the power of the potion they would see clear. To him who has looked upon the night of death and known its secret sweets, to him day never can be aught but vain, nor can he know a longing save for night, eternal, real, in which he is made one with love.

O night of love sink downwards and enfold them, grant them the oblivion they crave, release them from this world of partings and betrayals. Lo, the last light is quenched. Fancy and thought alike are lost, merged in the mystic shade that spread its wings of healing above their madness and despair. 'Now when deceitful daylight pales, when my raptured eye grows dim, then all that from which the light of day would shut my sight, seeking to blind me with false show, to the stanchless torments of my longing soul – then, ah, then, O wonder of fulfilment, even then I am the world!' Followed Brangäne's dark notes of warning, and then those soaring violins so higher than all reason.

'I cannot understand it all, Herr Spinell. Much of it I only divine. What does it mean, this "even then I am the world"?'

He explained, in a few low-toned words.

'Yes, yes. It means that. How is it you can understand it all so well, yet cannot play it?'

Strangely enough, he was not proof against this simple question. He coloured, twisted his hands together, shrank into his chair.

'The two things seldom happen together,' he wrung from his lips at last. 'No, I cannot play. But go on.'

And on they went, into the intoxicated music of the love-mystery. Did love ever die? Tristan's love? The love of thy Isolde, and of mine? Ah, no, death cannot touch that which can never die – and what of him could die, save what distracts and tortures love and severs united lovers? Love joined the two in sweet conjunction, death was powerless to sever such a bond, save only when death was given to one with the very life of the other. Their voices rose in mystic unison, rapt in the wordless hope of that death-in-love, of endless oneness in the wonder-kingdom of the night. Sweet night! Eternal night of love! And all-encompassing land of rapture! Once envisaged or divined, what eye could bear to open again on desolate dawn? Forfend such fears, most gentle death! Release these lovers quite from need of waking. Oh, tumultuous storm of rhythms! Oh, glad chromatic upward surge of meta-physical perception! How find, how bind this bliss so far remote from parting's torturing pangs? Ah, gentle glow of longing, soothing and kind, ah, yielding sweet-sublime, ah, raptured sinking into the twilight of eternity! Thou Isolde, Tristan I, yet no more Tristan, no more Isolde. . . .

All at once something startling happened. The musician broke off and peered into the darkness with her hand above her eyes. Herr Spinell turned round quickly in his chair. The corridor door had opened, a sinister form appeared, leant on the arm of a second form. It was a guest of Einfried, one of those who, like themselves, had been in no state to undertake the sleigh-ride, but had passed this twilight hour in one of her pathetic, instinctive rounds of the house. It was that patient who had borne fourteen children and was no longer capable of a single thought; it was Frau Pastor Höhlenrauch, on the arm of her nurse. She did not look up; with groping step she paced the dim background of the room and vanished by the opposite door, rigid and still, like a lost and wandering soul. Stillness reigned once more.

'That was Frau Pastor Höhlenrauch,' he said.

'Yes, that was poor Frau Höhlenrauch,' she answered. Then she turned over some leaves and played the finale, played Isolde's song of love and death.

How colourless and clear were her lips, how deep the shadows lay beneath her eyes! The little pale-blue vein in her transparent brow showed fearfully plain and prominent. Beneath her flying fingers the music mounted to its unbelievable climax and was resolved in that ruthless, sudden *pianissimo* which is like having the ground glide from beneath one's feet, yet like a sinking too into the very deeps of desire. Followed the immeasurable plenitude of that vast redemption and fulfilment; it was repeated, swelled into a deafening, unquenchable tumult of immense appeasement that wove and welled and seemed about to die away, only to swell again and weave the *Sehnsuchtsmotiv* into its harmony; at length to breathe an outward breath and die, faint on the air, and soar away. Profound stillness.

They both listened, their heads on one side.

'Those are bells,' she said.

'It is the sleighs,' he said. 'I will go now.'

He rose and walked across the room. At the door he halted, then turned and shifted uneasily from one foot to the other. And then, some fifteen or twenty paces from her, it came to pass that he fell upon his knees, both knees, without a sound. His long black coat spread out on the floor. He held his hands clasped over his mouth, and his shoulders heaved.

She sat there with hands in her lap, leaning forward, turned away from the piano, and looked at him. Her face wore a distressed, uncertain smile, while her eyes searched the dimness at the back of the room, searched so painfully, so dreamily, she seemed hardly able to focus her gaze.

The jingling of sleigh-bells came nearer and nearer, there was the crack of whips, a babel of voices.

The sleighing party had taken place on the twenty-sixth of February, and was talked of for long afterwards. The next day, February twenty-seventh, a day of thaw, that set everything to melting and dripping, splashing and running, Herr Klöterjahn's wife was in capital health and spirits. On the twenty-eighth she brought up a little blood – not much, still it was blood, and accompanied by far greater loss of strength than ever before. She went to bed.

Dr Leander examined her, stony-faced. He prescribed according to the dictates of science – morphia, little pieces of ice, absolute quiet. Next day, on account of pressure of work, he turned her case over to Dr Müller, who took it on in humility and meekness of spirit and according to the letter of his contract – a quiet, pallid, insignificant little man, whose unadvertised activities were consecrated to the care of the slight cases and the hopeless ones.

Dr Müller presently expressed the view that the separation between Frau Klöterjahn and her spouse had lasted overlong. It would be well if Herr Klöterjahn, in case his flourishing business permitted, were to make another visit to Einfried. One might write him – or even wire. And surely it would benefit the young mother's health and spirits if he were to bring young Anton with him – quite aside from the pleasure it would give the physicians to behold with their own eyes this so healthy little Anton.

And Herr Klöterjahn came. He got Herr Müller's little wire and arrived from the Baltic coast. He got out of the carriage, ordered coffee and rolls, and looked considerably aggrieved.

'My dear sir,' he asked, 'what is the matter? Why have I been summoned?'

'Because it is desirable that you should be near your wife,' Dr Müller replied.

'Desirable! Desirable! But is it *necessary*? It is a question of expense with me – times are poor and railway journeys cost money. Was it imperative I should take this whole day's journey? If it were the lungs that are attacked, I should say nothing. But as it is only the trachea, thank God – –'

'Herr Klöterjahn,' said Dr Müller mildly, 'in the first place the trachea is an important organ. . . .' He ought not to have said 'in the first place', because he did not go on to the second.

But there also arrived at Einfried, in Herr Klöterjahn's company, a full-figured personage arrayed all in red and gold and plaid, and she it was who carried on her arm Anton Klöterjahn, junior, that healthy little Anton. Yes, there he was, and nobody could deny that he was healthy even to excess. Pink and white and plump and fragrant, in fresh and immaculate attire, he rested heavily upon the bare red arm of his bebraided body-servant, consumed huge quantities of milk and chopped beef, shouted and screamed, and in every way surrendered himself to his instincts.

Our author from the window of his chamber had seen him arrive. With a peculiar gaze, both veiled and piercing, he fixed young Anton with his eye as he was carried from the carriage into the house. He stood there a long time with the same expression on his face.

Herr Spinell was sitting in his room 'at work'.

His room was like all the others at Einfried – old-fashioned, simple, and distinguished. The massive chest of drawers was mounted with brass lions' heads; the tall mirror on the wall was not a single surface, but made up of many little panes set in lead. There was no carpet on the polished blue paved floor, the stiff legs of the furniture prolonged themselves on it in clear-cut shadows. A spacious writing-table stood at the window, across whose panes the author had drawn the folds of a yellow curtain, in all probability that he might feel more retired.

In the yellow twilight he bent over the table and wrote – wrote one of those numerous letters which he sent weekly to the post and to which, quaintly enough, he seldom or never received an answer. A large, thick quire of paper lay before him, in whose upper left-hand corner was a curious involved drawing of a landscape and the name Detlev Spinell in the very latest thing in lettering. He was covering the page with a small, painfully neat, and punctiliously traced script.

'Sir:' he wrote, 'I address the following lines to you because I cannot help it; because what I have to say so fills and shakes and tortures me, the words come in such a rush, that I should choke if I did not take this means to relieve myself.'

If the truth were told, this about the rush of words was quite simply wide of the fact. And God knows what sort of vanity it was made Herr Spinell put it down. For his words did not come in a rush; they came with such pathetic slowness, considering the man was a writer by trade, you would have drawn the conclusion, watching him, that a writer is one to whom writing comes harder than to anybody else.

He held between two finger-tips one of those curious downy hairs he had on his cheek, and twirled it round and round, whole quarter-hours at a time, gazing into space and not coming forwards by a single line; then wrote a few words, daintily, and stuck again. Yet so much was true: that what had managed to get written sounded fluent and vigorous, though the matter was odd enough, even almost equivocal, and at times impossible to follow.

'I feel,' the letter went on, 'an imperative necessity to make you see what I see ; to show you through my eyes, illuminated by the same power of language that clothes them for me, all the things which have stood before my inner eye for weeks, like an indelible vision. It is my habit to yield to the impulse which urges me to put my own experiences into flamingly right and unforgettable words and to give them to the world. And therefore hear me.

'I will do no more than relate what has been and what is: I will merely tell a story, a brief, unspeakably touching story, without comment, blame, or passing of judgement; simply in my own words. It is the story of Gabriele Eckhof, of the woman whom you, sir, call your wife – and mark you this: it is your story, it happened to you, yet it will be I who will for the first time lift it for you to the level of an experience.

'Do you remember the garden, the old, overgrown garden behind the grey patrician house? The moss was green in the crannies of its weather-beaten wall, and behind the wall dreams and neglect held sway. Do you remember the fountain in the centre? The pale mauve lilies leaned over its crumbling rim, the little stream prattled softly as it fell upon the riven paving. The summer day was drawing to its close.

'Seven maidens sat circlewise round the fountain; but the seventh, or rather the first and only one, was not like the others, for the sinking sun seemed to be weaving a queenly coronal among her locks. Her eyes were like troubled dreams, and yet her pure lips wore a smile.

'They were singing. They lifted their little faces to the leaping streamlet and watched its charming curve droop earthward – their music hovered round it as it leaped and danced. Perhaps their slim hands were folded in their laps the while they sang.

'Can you, sir, recall the scene? Or did you ever see it? No, you saw it not. Your eyes were not formed to see it nor your ears to catch the chaste music of their song. You saw it not, or else you would have forbidden your lungs to breathe, your heart to beat. You must have turned aside and gone back to your own life taking with you what you had seen to preserve it in the depth of your soul to the end of your earthly life, a sacred and inviolable relic. But what did you do?

'That scene, sir, was an end and culmination. Why did you come to spoil it, to give it a sequel, to turn it into the channels of ugly and commonplace life? It was a peaceful apotheosis and a moving, bathed in a sunset beauty of decadence, decay, and death. An ancient stock, too exhausted and refined for life and action, stood there at the end of its days; its late manifestations were those of art: violin notes, full of that melancholy understanding which is ripeness for death. . . . Did you look into her eyes – those eyes where tears so often stood, lured by the dying sweetness of the violin? Her six friends may have had souls that belonged to life; but hers, the queen's and sister's, death and beauty had claimed for their own.

'You saw it, that deathly beauty; saw, and coveted. The sight of that touching purity moved you with no awe or trepidation. And it was not enough for you to see, you must possess, you must use, you must desecrate. . . . It was the refinement of a choice you made – you are a gourmand, sir, a plebeian gourmand, a peasant with taste.

'Once more let me say that I have no wish to offend you. What I have just said is not an affront; it is a statement, a simple, psychological statement of your simple personality – a personality which for literary purposes is entirely uninteresting. I make the statement solely because I feel an impulse to clarify for you your own thoughts and actions; because it is my inevitable task on this earth to call things by their right names, to make them speak, to illuminate the unconscious. The world is full of what I call the unconscious type, and I cannot endure it; I cannot endure all these unconscious types! I cannot bear all this dull, uncomprehending, unperceiving living and behaving, this world of maddening *naïveté* about me! It tortures me until I am driven irresistibly to set it all in relief, in the round, to explain, express and make self-conscious everything in the world – so far as my powers will reach – quite unhampered by the result, whether it be for good or evil, whether it brings consolation and healing or piles grief on grief.

'You, sir, as I said, are a plebeian gourmand, a peasant with taste. You stand upon an extremely low evolutionary level; you own constitution is coarse-fibred. But wealth and a sedentary habit of life have brought about in you a corruption of the nervous system, as sudden as it is unhistoric; and this corruption has been accompanied by a lascivious refinement in your choice of gratifications. It is altogether possible that the muscles of your gullet began to contract, as at the sight of some particularly rare dish, when you conceived the idea of making Gabriele Eckhof your own.

'In short, you lead her idle will astray, you beguile her out of that moss-grown garden into the ugliness of life, you give her your own vulgar name and make of her a married woman, a housewife, a mother. You take that deathly beauty – spent, aloof, flowering in lofty unconcern of the uses of this world – and debase it to the service of common things, you sacrifice it to that stupid, contemptible, clumsy graven image we call "nature" – and not the faintest suspicion of the vileness of your conduct visits your peasant soul.

'Again. What is the result? This being, whose eyes are like troubled dreams, she bears you a child; and so doing she endows the new life, a gross continuation of its author's own, with all the blood, all the physical energy she possesses – and she dies. She dies, sir! And if she does not go hence with your vulgarity upon her head; if at the very last she has lifted herself out of the depths of degradation, and passes in an ecstasy, with the deathly kiss of beauty on her brow – well, it is I, sir, who have seen to that! You, meanwhile, were probably spending your time with chambermaids in dark corners.

'But your son, Gabriele Eckhof's son, is alive; he is living and flourishing. Perhaps he will continue in the way of his father, become a well-fed, trading, tax-paying citizen; a capable, philistine pillar of society; in any case, a tone-deaf, normally functioning individual, responsible, sturdy, and stupid, troubled by not a doubt.

'Kindly permit me to tell you, sir, that I hate you. I hate you and your child, as I hate the life of which you are the representative: cheap, ridiculous, but yet triumphant life, the everlasting antipodes and deadly enemy of beauty. I cannot say I despise you – for I am honest. You are stronger than I. I have no armour for the struggle between us, I have only the Word, avenging weapon of the weak. To-day I have availed myself of this weapon. This letter is nothing but an act of revenge – you see how honourable I am – and if any word of mine is sharp and bright and beautiful enough to strike home, to make you feel the presence of a power you do not know, to shake even a minute your robust equilibrium, I shall rejoice indeed. – DETLEV SPINELL.'

And Herr Spinell put this screed into an envelope, applied a stamp and a many-flourished address, and committed it to the post.

Herr Klöterjahn knocked on Herr Spinell's door. He carried a sheet of paper in his hand covered with neat script and he looked like a man bent on energetic action. The post office had done its duty, the letter had taken its appointed way: it had travelled from Einfried to Einfried and reached the hand for which it was meant. It was now four o'clock in the afternoon.

Herr Klöterjahn's entry found Herr Spinell sitting on the sofa reading his own novel with the appalling cover-design. He rose and gave his caller a surprised and inquiring look, though at the same time he distinctly flushed.

'Good afternoon,' said Herr Klöterjahn. 'Pardon the interruption. But may I ask if you wrote this?' He held up in his left hand the sheet inscribed with fine clear characters and struck it with the back of his right and made it crackle. Then he stuffed that hand into the pocket of his easy-fitting trousers, put his head on one side, and opened his mouth, in a way some people have, to listen.

Herr Spinell, curiously enough, smiled; he smiled engagingly, with a rather confused, apologetic air. He put his hand to his head as though trying to recollect himself, and said:

'Ah! – yes, quite right, I took the liberty – –'

The fact was, he had given in to his natural man to-day and slept nearly up to midday, with the result that he was suffering from a bad conscience and a heavy head, was nervous and incapable of putting up a fight. And the spring air made him limp and good-for-nothing. So much we must say in extenuation of the utterly silly figure he cut in the interview which followed.

'Ah? Indeed! Very good!' said Herr Klöterjahn. He dug his chin into his chest, elevated his brows, stretched his arms, and indulged in various other antics by way of getting down to business after his introductory question. But unfortunately he so much enjoyed the figure he cut that he rather overshot the mark, and the rest of the scene hardly lived up to this preliminary pantomime. However, Herr Spinell went rather pale.

'Very good!' repeated Herr Klöterjahn. 'Then permit me to give you an answer in person; it strikes me as idiotic to write pages of letter to a person when you can speak to him any hour of the day.'

'Well, idiotic . . .' Herr Spinell said, with his apologetic smile. He sounded almost meek.

'Idiotic!' repeated Herr Klöterjahn, nodding violently in token of the soundness of his position. 'And I should not demean myself to answer this scrawl; to tell the truth, I should have thrown it away at once if I had not found in it the explanation of certain changes – however, that is no affair of yours, and has nothing to do with the thing anyhow. I am a man of action, I have other things to do than to think about your unspeakable visions.'

'I wrote "*indelible vision*,"' said Herr Spinell, drawing himself up. This was the only moment at which he displayed a little self-respect.

'Indelible, unspeakable,' responded Herr Klöterjahn, referring to the text. 'You write a villainous hand, sir; you would not get a position in my office, let me tell you. It looks clear enough at first, but when you come to study it, it is full of shakes and quavers. But that is your affair, it's no business of mine. What I have come to say to you is that you are a tom-fool – which you probably know already. Furthermore, you are a cowardly sneak; I don't suppose I have to give the evidence for that either. My wife wrote me once that when you meet a woman you don't look her square in the face, but just give her a side squint, so as to carry away a good impression, because you are afraid of the reality. I should probably have heard more of the same sort of stories about you, only unfortunately she stopped mentioning you. But this is the kind of thing you are: you talk so much about "beauty"; you are all chicken-livered hypocrisy and cant – which is probably at the bottom of your impudent allusion to out-of-the-way corners too. That ought to crush me, of course, but it just makes me laugh – it doesn't do a thing but make me laugh! Understand? Have I clarified your thoughts and actions for you, you pitiable object, you? Though of course it is not my invariable calling – –'

'"*Inevitable*" was the word I used,' Herr Spinell said; but he did not insist on the point. He stood there, crestfallen, like a big, unhappy, chidden, grey-haired schoolboy.

'Invariable or inevitable, whichever you like – anyhow you are a contemptible cur, and that I tell you. You see me every day at table, you bow and smirk and say good-morning – and one fine day you send me a scrawl full of idiotic abuse. Yes, you've a lot of courage – on paper! And it's not only this ridiculous letter – you have been intriguing behind my back. I can see that now. Though you need not flatter yourself it did any good. If you imagine you put any ideas into my wife's head you never were more mistaken in your life. And if you think she behaved any differently when we came from what she always does, then you just put the cap onto your own foolishness. She did not kiss the little chap, that's true, but it was only a precaution, because they have the idea now that the trouble is with her lungs, and in such cases you can't tell whether – though that still remains to be proved, no matter what you say with your "She dies, sir," you silly ass!'

Here Herr Klöterjahn paused for breath. He was in a furious passion; he kept stabbing the air with his right forefinger and crumpling the sheet of paper in his other hand. His face, between the blond English mutton-chops, was frightfully red and his dark brow was rent with swollen veins like lightnings of scorn.

'You hate me,' he went on, 'and you would despise me if I were not stronger than you. Yes, you're right there! I've got my heart in the right place, by God, and you've got yours mostly in the seat of your trousers. I would most certainly hack you into bits if it weren't against the law, you and your gabble about the "Word", you skulking fool! But I have no intention of putting up with your insults; and when I show this part about the vulgar name to my lawyer at home, you will very likely get a little surprise. My name, sir, is a first-rate name, and I have made it so by my own efforts. You know better than I do whether anybody would ever lend you a penny piece on yours, you lazy lout! The law defends people against the kind you are! You are a common danger, you are enough to drive a body crazy! But you're left this time, my master! I don't let individuals like you get the best of me so fast! I've got my heart in the right place – –'.

Herr Klöterjahn's excitement had really reached a pitch. He shrieked, he bellowed, over and over again, that his heart was in the right place.

'"They were singing." Exactly. Well, they weren't. They were knitting. And if I heard what they said, it was about a recipe for potato pancakes; and when I show my father-in-law that about the old decayed family you'll probably have a libel suit on your hands. "Did you see the picture?" Yes, of course I saw it; only I don't see why that should make me hold my breath and run away. I don't leer at women out of the corner of my eye; I look at them square, and if I like their looks I go for them. I have my heart in the right place – –'

Somebody knocked. Knocked eight or ten times, quite fast, one after the other – a sudden, alarming little commotion that made Herr Klöterjahn pause; and an unsteady voice that kept tripping over itself in its haste and distress said:

'Herr Klöterjahn, Herr Klöterjahn – oh, is Herr Klöterjahn there?'

'Stop outside,' said Herr Klöterjahn, in a growl. . . . 'What's the matter? I'm busy talking.'

'Oh, Herr Klöterjahn,' said the quaking, breaking voice, 'you must come! The doctors are there too – oh, it is all so dreadfully sad – –'

He took one step to the door and tore it open. Frau Magistrate Spatz was standing there. She had her handkerchief before her mouth, and great egg-shaped tears rolled into it, two by two.

'Herr Klöterjahn,' she got out. 'It is so frightfully sad. . . . She has brought up so much blood, such a horrible lot of blood. . . . She was sitting up quite quietly in bed and humming a little snatch of music . . . and there it came . . . my God, such a quantity you never saw. . . .'

'Is she dead?' yelled Herr Klöterjahn. As he spoke he clutched the Rätin by the arm and pulled her to and fro on the sill. 'Not quite? Not dead; she can see me, can't she? Brought up a little blood again, from the lung, eh? Yes, I give

in, it may be from the lung. Gabriele!' he suddenly cried out,
and his eyes filled with tears; you could see what a burst of
good, warm, honest human feeling came over him. 'Yes, I'm
coming,' he said, and dragged the Rätin after him as he went
with long strides down the corridor. You could still hear his
voice, from quite a distance, sounding fainter and fainter:
'Not quite, eh? From the lung?'

Herr Spinell stood still on the spot where he had stood during
the whole of Herr Klöterjahn's rudely interrupted call and
looked out of the open door. At length he took a couple of
steps and listened down the corridor. But all was quiet, so he
closed the door and came back into the room.

He looked at himself awhile in the glass, then he went up to
the writing-table, took a little flask and a glass out of a drawer,
and drank a cognac – for which nobody can blame him. Then
he stretched himself out on the sofa and closed his eyes.

The upper half of the window was down. Outside in the
garden birds were twittering; those dainty, saucy little notes
held all the spring, finely and penetratingly expressed. Herr
Spinell spoke once: '*Invariable calling,*' he said, and moved his
head and drew in the air through his teeth as though his
nerves pained him violently.

Impossible to recover any poise or tranquillity. Crude experiences like this were too much – he was not made for them.
By a sequence of emotions, the analysis of which would lead
us too far afield, Herr Spinell arrived at the decision that it
would be well for him to have a little out-of-doors exercise.
He took his hat and went downstairs.

As he left the house and issued into the mild, fragrant air,
he turned his head and lifted his eyes, slowly, scanning the
house until he reached one of the windows, a curtained window, on which his gaze rested awhile, fixed and sombre.
Then he laid his hands on his back and moved away across the
gravel path. He moved in deep thought.

The beds were still straw-covered, the trees and bushes bare; but the snow was gone, the path was only damp in spots. The large garden with its grottoes, bowers and little pavilions lay in the splendid colourful afternoon light, strong shadow and rich, golden sun, and the dark network of branches stood out sharp and articulate against the bright sky.

It was about that hour of the afternoon when the sun takes shape, and from being a formless volume of light turns to a visibly sinking disk, whose milder, more saturated glow the eye can tolerate. Herr Spinell did not see the sun, the direction the path took hid it from his view. He walked with bent head and hummed a strain of music, a short phrase, a figure that mounted wailingly and complainingly upward – the *Sehnsuchtsmotiv*. . . . But suddenly, with a start, a quick, jerky intake of breath, he stopped, as though rooted to the path, and gazed straight ahead of him, with brows fiercely gathered, staring eyes, and an expression of horrified repulsion.

The path had curved just here, he was facing the setting sun. It stood large and slantwise in the sky, crossed by two narrow strips of gold-rimmed cloud; it set the tree-tops aglow and poured its red-gold radiance across the garden. And there, erect in the path, in the midst of the glory, with the sun's mighty aureola above her head, there confronted him an exuberant figure, all arrayed in red and gold and plaid. She had one hand on her swelling hip, with the other she moved to and fro the graceful little perambulator. And in this perambulator sat the child – sat Anton Klöterjahn, junior, Gabriele Eckhof's fat son.

There he sat among his cushions, in a woolly white jacket and large white hat, plump-cheeked, well cared for, and magnificent; and his blithe unerring gaze encountered Herr Spinell's. The novelist pulled himself together. Was he not a man, had he not the power to pass this unexpected, sunkindled apparition there in the path and continue on his walk? But Anton Klöterjahn began to laugh and shout – most hor-

rible to see. He squealed, he crowed with inconceivable delight
– it was positively uncanny to hear him.

God knows what had taken him; perhaps the sight of Herr
Spinell's long, black figure set him off; perhaps an attack of
sheer animal spirits gave rise to his wild outburst of merriment.
He had a bone teething-ring in one hand and a tin rattle in the
other; and these two objects he flung aloft with shoutings,
shook them to and fro, and clashed them together in the air, as
though purposely to frighten Herr Spinell. His eyes were
almost shut. His mouth gaped open till all the rosy gums were
displayed; and as he shouted he rolled his head about in excess
of mirth.

Herr Spinell turned round and went thence. Pursued by the
youthful Klöterjahn's joyous screams he went away across
the gravel, walking stiffly, yet not without grace; his gait was
the hesitating gait of one who would disguise the fact that,
inwardly, he is running away.

1902

TONIO KRÖGER

*

THE WINTER sun, poor ghost of itself, hung milky and wan behind layers of cloud above the huddled roofs of the town. In the gabled streets it was wet and windy and there came in gusts a sort of soft hail, not ice, not snow.

School was out. The hosts of the released streamed over the paved court and out at the wrought-iron gate, where they broke up and hastened off right and left. Elder pupils held their books in a strap high on the left shoulder and rowed, right arm against the wind, towards dinner. Small people trotted gaily off, splashing the slush with their feet, the tools of learning rattling amain in their walrus-skin satchels. But one and all pulled off their caps and cast down their eyes in awe before the Olympian hat and ambrosial beard of a master moving homewards with measured stride. . . .

'Ah, there you are at last, Hans,' said Tonio Kröger. He had been waiting a long time in the street and went up with a smile to the friend he saw coming out of the gate in talk with other boys and about to go off with them. . . . 'What?' said Hans, and looked at Tonio. 'Right-oh! We'll take a little walk, then.'

Tonio said nothing and his eyes were clouded. Did Hans forget, had he only just remembered that they were to take a walk together to-day? And he himself had looked forward to it with almost incessant joy.

'Well, good-bye, fellows,' said Hans Hansen to his comrades. 'I'm taking a walk with Kröger.' And the two turned to their left, while the others sauntered off in the opposite direction.

Hans and Tonio had time to take a walk after school because

in neither of their families was dinner served before four o'clock. Their fathers were prominent business men, who held public office and were of consequence in the town. Hans's people had owned for some generations the big wood-yards down by the river, where powerful machine-saws hissed and spat and cut up timber; while Tonio was the son of Consul Kröger, whose grain-sacks with the firm's name in great black letters you might see any day driven through the streets; his large, old ancestral home was the finest house in all the town. The two friends had to keep taking off their hats to their many acquaintances; some folk did not even wait for the fourteen-year-old lads to speak first, as by rights they should.

Both of them carried their satchels across their shoulders and both were well and warmly dressed: Hans in a short sailor jacket, with the wide blue collar of his sailor suit turned out over shoulders and back, and Tonio in a belted grey overcoat. Hans wore a Danish sailor cap with black ribbons, beneath which streamed a shock of straw-coloured hair. He was uncommonly handsome and well built, broad in the shoulders and narrow in the hips, with keen, far-apart, steel-blue eyes; while beneath Tonio's round fur cap was a brunette face with the finely chiselled features of the south; the dark eyes, with delicate shadows and too heavy lids, looked dreamily and a little timorously on the world. Tonio's walk was idle and uneven, whereas the other's slim legs in their black stockings moved with an elastic, rhythmic tread.

Tonio did not speak. He suffered. His rather oblique brows were drawn together in a frown, his lips were rounded to whistle, he gazed into space with his head on one side. Posture and manner were habitual.

Suddenly Hans shoved his arm into Tonio's, with a sideways look – he knew very well what the trouble was. And Tonio, though he was silent for the next few steps, felt his heart soften.

'I hadn't forgotten, you see, Tonio,' Hans said, gazing at

the pavement. 'I only thought it wouldn't come off to-day because it was so wet and windy. But I don't mind that at all, and it's jolly of you to have waited. I thought you had gone home, and I was cross. . . .'

Everything in Tonio leaped and jumped for joy at the words.

'All right; let's go over the wall,' he said with a quaver in his voice. 'Over the Millwall and the Holstenwall, and I'll go as far as your house with you, Hans. Then I'll have to walk back alone, but that doesn't matter; next time you can go round my way.'

At bottom he was not really convinced by what Hans said; he quite knew the other attached less importance to this walk than he did himself. Yet he saw Hans was sorry for his remissness and willing to be put in a position to ask pardon, a pardon that Tonio was far indeed from withholding.

The truth was, Tonio loved Hans Hansen, and had already suffered much on his account. He who loves the more is the inferior and must suffer; in this hard and simple fact his fourteen-year-old soul had already been instructed by life; and he was so organized that he received such experiences consciously, wrote them down as it were inwardly, and even, in a certain way, took pleasure in them, though without ever letting them mould his conduct, indeed, or drawing any practical advantage from them. Being what he was, he found this knowledge far more important and far more interesting than the sort they made him learn in school; yes, during his lesson hours in the vaulted Gothic classrooms he was mainly occupied in feeling his way about among these intuitions of his and penetrating them. The process gave him the same kind of satisfaction as that he felt when he moved about in his room with his violin – for he played the violin – and made the tones, brought out as softly as ever he knew how, mingle with the plashing of the fountain that leaped and danced down there in the garden beneath the branches of the old walnut tree.

The fountain, the old walnut tree, his fiddle, and away in the distance, the North Sea, within sound of whose summer murmurings he spent his holidays – these were the things he loved, within these he enfolded his spirit, among these things his inner life took its course. And they were all things whose names were effective in verse and occurred pretty frequently in the lines Tonio Kröger sometimes wrote.

The fact that he had a note-book full of such things, written by himself, leaked out through his own carelessness and injured him no little with the masters as well as among his fellows. On the one hand, Consul Kröger's son found their attitude both cheap and silly, and despised his schoolmates and his masters as well, and in his turn (with extraordinary penetration) saw through and disliked their personal weaknesses and bad breeding. But then, on the other hand, he himself felt his verse-making extravagant and out of place and to a certain extent agreed with those who considered it an unpleasing occupation. But that did not enable him to leave off.

As he wasted his time at home, was slow and absent-minded at school, and always had bad marks from the masters, he was in the habit of bringing home pitifully poor reports, which troubled and angered his father, a tall, fastidiously dressed man with thoughtful blue eyes, and always a wild flower in his buttonhole. But for his mother, she cared nothing about the reports – Tonio's beautiful black-haired mother, whose name was Consuelo, and who was so absolutely different from the other ladies in the town, because father had brought her long ago from some place far down on the map.

Tonio loved his dark, fiery mother, who played the piano and mandolin so wonderfully, and he was glad his doubtful standing among men did not distress her. Though at the same time he found his father's annoyance a more dignified and respectable attitude and despite his scoldings understood him very well, whereas his mother's blithe indifference always seemed just a little wanton. His thoughts at times would run something like this: 'It is true enough that I am what I am and will not and cannot alter: heedless, self-willed, with my mind on things nobody else thinks of. And so it is right they should scold and punish me and not smother things all up with kisses and music. After all, we are not gypsies living in a green wagon; we're respectable people, the family of Consul Kröger.' And not seldom he would think: 'Why is it I am different, why do I fight everything, why am I at odds with the masters and like a stranger among the other boys? The good scholars, and the solid majority – they don't find the masters funny, they don't write verses, their thoughts are all about things that people do think about and can talk about out loud. How regular and comfortable they must feel, knowing that everybody knows just where they stand! It must be nice! But what is the matter with me, and what will be the end of it all?'

These thoughts about himself and his relation to life played an important part in Tonio's love for Hans Hansen. He loved him in the first place because he was handsome; but in the next because he was in every respect his own opposite and foil. Hans Hansen was a capital scholar, and a jolly chap to boot, who was head at drill, rode and swam to perfection, and lived in the sunshine of popularity. The masters were almost tender with him, they called him Hans and were partial to him in every way; the other pupils curried favour with him; even grown people stopped him in the street, twitched the shock of hair beneath his Danish sailor cap, and said: 'Ah, here you are, Hans Hansen, with your pretty blond hair! Still head of the school? Remember me to your father and mother, that's a fine lad!'

Such was Hans Hansen; and ever since Tonio Kröger had known him, from the very minute he set eyes on him, he had burned inwardly with a heavy, envious longing. 'Who else has blue eyes like yours, or lives in such friendliness and harmony with all the world? You are always spending your time with some right and proper occupation. When you have done your prep you take your riding-lesson, or make things with a fret-saw; even in the holidays, at the seashore, you row and sail and swim all the time, while I wander off somewhere and lie down in the sand and stare at the strange and mysterious changes that whisk over the face of the sea. And all that is why your eyes are so clear. To be like you . . .'

He made no attempt to be like Hans Hansen, and perhaps hardly even seriously wanted to. What he did ardently, painfully want was that just as he was, Hans Hansen should love him; and he wooed Hans Hansen in his own way, deeply, lingeringly, devotedly, with a melancholy that gnawed and burned more terribly than all the sudden passion one might have expected from his exotic looks.

And he wooed not in vain. Hans respected Tonio's superior power of putting certain difficult matters into words; moreover, he felt the lively presence of an uncommonly strong and tender feeling for himself; he was grateful for it, and his response gave Tonio much happiness – though also many pangs of jealousy and disillusion over his futile efforts to establish a communion of spirit between them. For the queer thing was that Tonio, who after all envied Hans Hansen for being what he was, still kept on trying to draw him over to his own side; though of course he could succeed in this at most only at moments and superficially. . . .

'I have just been reading something so wonderful and splendid . . .' he said. They were walking and eating together out of a bag of fruit toffees they had bought at Iverson's sweet-shop in Mill Street for ten pfennigs. 'You must read it, Hans, it is Schiller's *Don Carlos* . . . I'll lend it you if you like. . . .'

'Oh, no,' said Hans Hansen, 'you needn't, Tonio, that's not anything for me. I'll stick to my horse books. There are wonderful cuts in them, let me tell you. I'll show them to you when you come to see me. They are instantaneous photography – the horse in motion; you can see him trot and canter and jump, in all positions, that you never can get to see in life, because they happen so fast. . . .'

'In all positions?' asked Tonio politely. 'Yes, that must be great. But about *Don Carlos* – it is beyond anything you could possibly dream of. There are places in it that are so lovely they make you jump . . . as though it were an explosion – –'

'An explosion?' asked Hans Hansen. 'What sort of an explosion?'

'For instance, the place where the king has been crying because the marquis betrayed him . . . but the marquis did it only out of love for the prince, you see, he sacrifices himself for his sake. And the word comes out of the cabinet into the antechamber that the king has been weeping. "Weeping? The king been weeping?" All the courtiers are fearfully upset, it goes through and through you, for the king has always been so frightfully stiff and stern. But it is so easy to understand why he cried, and I feel sorrier for him than for the prince and the marquis put together. He is always so alone, nobody loves him, and then he thinks he has found one man, and then *he* betrays him . . . .'

Hans Hansen looked sideways into Tonio's face, and something in it must have won him to the subject, for suddenly he shoved his arm once more into Tonio's and said:

'How had he betrayed him, Tonio?'

Tonio went on.

'Well,' he said, 'you see all the letters for Brabant and Flanders – –'

'There comes Irwin Immerthal,' said Hans.

Tonio stopped talking. If only the earth would open and swallow Immerthal up! 'Why does he have to come disturbing us? If he only doesn't go with us all the way and talk about the riding-lessons!' For Irwin Immerthal had riding-lessons too. He was the son of the bank president and lived close by, outside the city wall. He had already been home and left his bag, and now he walked towards them through the avenue. His legs were crooked and his eyes like slits.

"'lo, Immerthal,' said Hans. 'I'm taking a little walk with Kröger. . . .'

'I have to go into town on an errand,' said Immerthal. 'But I'll walk a little way with you. Are those fruit toffees you've got? Thanks, I'll have a couple. To-morrow we have our next lesson, Hans.' He meant the riding-lesson.

'What larks!' said Hans. 'I'm going to get the leather gaiters for a present, because I was top lately in our papers.'

'You don't take riding-lessons, I suppose, Kröger?' asked Immerthal, and his eyes were only two gleaming cracks.

'No . . .' answered Tonio, uncertainly.

'You ought to ask your father,' Hans Hansen remarked, 'so you could have lessons too, Kröger.'

'Yes . . .' said Tonio. He spoke hastily and without interest; his throat had suddenly contracted, because Hans had called him by his last name. Hans seemed conscious of it too, for he said by way of explanation: 'I call you Kröger because your first name is so crazy. Don't mind my saying so, I can't do with it at all. Tonio – why, what sort of name is that? Though of course I know it's not your fault in the least.'

'No, they probably called you that because it sounds so foreign and sort of something special,' said Immerthal, obviously with intent to say just the right thing.

Tonio's mouth twitched. He pulled himself together and said:

'Yes, it's a silly name – Lord knows I'd rather be called Heinrich or Wilhelm. It's all because I'm named after my mother's brother Antonio. She comes from down there, you know. . . .'

There he stopped and let the others have their say about horses and saddles. Hans had taken Immerthal's arm; he talked with a fluency that *Don Carlos* could never have roused in him. . . . Tonio felt a mounting desire to weep pricking his nose from time to time; he had hard work to control the trembling of his lips.

Hans could not stand his name – what was to be done? He himself was called Hans, and Immerthal was called Irwin; two good, sound, familiar names, offensive to nobody. And Tonio was foreign and queer. Yes, there was always something queer about him, whether he would or no, and he was alone, the regular and usual would none of him; although after all he was no gypsy in a green wagon, but the son of Consul Kröger, a member of the Kröger family. But why did Hans call him Tonio as long as they were alone and then feel ashamed as soon as anybody else was by? Just now he had won him over, they had been close together, he was sure. 'How had he betrayed him, Tonio?' Hans asked, and took his arm. But he had breathed easier directly Immerthal came up, he had dropped him like a shot, even gratuitously taunted him with his outlandish name. How it hurt to have to see through all this! . . . Hans Hansen did like him a little, when they were alone, that he knew. But let a third person come, he was ashamed, and offered up his friend. And again he was alone. He thought of King Philip. The king had wept. . . .

'Goodness, I have to go,' said Irwin Immerthal. 'Good-bye and thanks for the toffee.' He jumped upon a bench that stood by the way, ran along it with his crooked legs, jumped down and trotted off.

'I like Immerthal,' said Hans, with emphasis. He had a spoilt and arbitrary way of announcing his likes and dislikes, as though graciously pleased to confer them like an order on this person and that. . . . He went on talking about the riding-lessons where he had left off. Anyhow, it was not very much farther to his house; the walk over the walls was not a long one. They held their caps and bent their heads before the strong, damp wind that rattled and groaned in the leafless trees. And Hans Hansen went on talking, Tonio throwing in a forced yes or no from time to time. Hans talked eagerly, had taken his arm again; but the contact gave Tonio no pleasure. The nearness was only apparent, not real; it meant nothing. . . .

They struck away from the walls close to the station, where they saw a train puff busily past, idly counted the coaches, and waved to the man who was perched on top of the last one bundled in a leather coat. They stopped in front of the Hansen villa on the Lindenplatz, and Hans went into detail about what fun it was to stand on the bottom rail of the garden and let it swing on its creaking hinges. After that they said good-bye.

'I must go in now,' said Hans. 'Good-bye, Tonio. Next time I'll take you home, see if I don't.'

'Good-bye, Hans,' said Tonio. 'It was a nice walk.'

They put out their hands, all wet and rusty from the garden gate. But as Hans looked into Tonio's eyes, he bethought himself, a look of remorse came over his charming face.

'And I'll read *Don Carlos* pretty soon, too,' he said quickly. 'That bit about the king in his cabinet must be nuts.' Then he took his bag under his arm and ran off through the front garden. Before he disappeared he turned and nodded once more.

And Tonio went off as though on wings. The wind was at his back; but it was not the wind alone that bore him along so lightly.

Hans would read *Don Carlos*, and then they would have something to talk about, and neither Irwin Immerthal nor another could join in. How well they understood each other! Perhaps – who knew? – some day he might even get Hans to write poetry! . . . No, no, that he did not ask. Hans must not become like Tonio, he must stop just as he was, so strong and bright, everybody loved him as he was, and Tonio most of all. But it would do him no harm to read *Don Carlos*. . . . Tonio passed under the squat old city gate, along by the harbour, and up the steep, wet, windy, gabled street to his parents' house. His heart beat richly: longing was awake in it, and a gentle envy; a faint contempt, and no little innocent bliss.

Ingeborg Holm, blonde little Inge, the daughter of Dr Holm, who lived on Market Square opposite the tall old Gothic fountain with its manifold spires – she it was Tonio Kröger loved when he was sixteen years old.

Strange how things come about! He had seen her a thousand times; then one evening he saw her again; saw her in a certain light, talking with a friend in a certain saucy way, laughing and tossing her head; saw her lift her arm and smooth her back hair with her schoolgirl hand, that was by no means particularly fine or slender, in such a way that the thin white sleeve slipped down from her elbow; heard her speak a word or two, a quite indifferent phrase, but with a certain intonation, with a warm ring in her voice; and his heart throbbed with ecstasy, far stronger than that he had once felt when he looked at Hans Hansen long ago, when he was still a little stupid boy.

That evening he carried away her picture in his eye: the thick blonde plait, the longish, laughing blue eyes, the saddle of pale freckles across the nose. He could not go to sleep for hearing that ring in her voice; he tried in a whisper to imitate the tone in which she had uttered the commonplace phrase, and felt a shiver run through and through him. He knew by experience that this was love. And he was accurately aware that love would surely bring him much pain, affliction, and sadness, that it would certainly destroy his peace, filling his heart to overflowing with melodies which would be no good to him because he would never have the time or tranquillity to give them permanent form. Yet he received this love with joy, surrendered himself to it, and cherished it with all the strength of his being; for he knew that love made one vital and rich, and he longed to be vital and rich, far more than he did to work tranquilly on anything to give it permanent form.

Tonio Kröger fell in love with merry Ingeborg Holm in Frau Consul Hustede's drawing-room on the evening when it was emptied of furniture for the weekly dancing-class. It was a private class, attended only by members of the first families; it met by turns in the various parental houses to receive instruction from Knaak, the dancing-master, who came from Hamburg expressly for the purpose.

François Knaak was his name, and what a man he was! '*J'ai l'honneur de me vous représenter*,' he would say, '*mon nom est Knaak*. . . . This is not said during the bowing, but after you have finished and are standing up straight again. In a low voice, but distinctly. Of course one does not need to introduce oneself in French every day in the week, but if you can do it correctly and faultlessly in French you are not likely to make a mistake when you do it in German.' How marvellously the silky black frock-coat fitted his chubby hips! His trouser-legs fell down in soft folds upon his patent-leather pumps with their wide satin bows, and his brown eyes glanced about him with languid pleasure in their own beauty.

All this excess of self-confidence and good form was positively overpowering. He went trippingly – and nobody tripped like him, so elastically, so weavingly, rockingly, royally – up to the mistress of the house, made a bow, waited for a hand to be put forth. This vouchsafed, he gave murmurous voice to his gratitude, stepped buoyantly back, turned on his left foot, swiftly drawing the right one backwards on its toe-tip and moved away with his hips shaking.

When you took leave of a company you must go backwards out at the door; when you fetched a chair, you were not to shove it along the floor or clutch it by one leg; but gently by the back, and set it down without a sound. When you stood you were not to fold your hands on your tummy or seek with your tongue the corners of your mouth. If you did, Herr Knaak had a way of showing you how it looked that filled you with disgust for that particular gesture all the rest of your life.

This was deportment. As for dancing, Herr Knaak was, if

possible, even more of a master at that. The salon was emptied of furniture and lighted by a gas-chandelier in the middle of the ceiling and candles on the mantel-shelf. The floor was strewn with talc, and the pupils stood about in a dumb semi-circle. But in the next room, behind the portières, mothers and aunts sat on plush-upholstered chairs and watched Herr Knaak through their lorgnettes, as in little springs and hops, curtsying slightly, the hem of his frock-coat held up on each side by two fingers, he demonstrated the single steps of the mazurka. When he wanted to dazzle his audience completely he would suddenly and unexpectedly spring from the ground, whirling his two legs about each other with bewildering swiftness in the air, as it were trilling with them, and then, with a subdued bump, which nevertheless shook everything within him to its depths, returned to earth.

'What an unmentionable monkey!' thought Tonio Kröger to himself. But he saw the absorbed smile on jolly little Inge's face as she followed Herr Knaak's movements; and that, though not that alone, roused in him something like admiration of all this wonderfully controlled corporeality. How tranquil, how imperturbable was Herr Knaak's gaze! His eyes did not plumb the depth of things to the place where life becomes complex and melancholy; they knew nothing save that they were beautiful brown eyes. But that was just why his bearing was so proud. To be able to walk like that, one must be stupid; then one was loved, then one was lovable. He could so well understand how it was that Inge, blonde, sweet little Inge, looked at Herr Knaak as she did. But would never a girl look at him like that?

Oh, yes, there would, and did. For instance, Magdalena Vermehren, Attorney Vermehren's daughter, with the gentle mouth and the great, dark, brilliant eyes, so serious and adoring. She often fell down in the dance; but when it was 'ladies' choice' she came up to him; she knew he wrote verses and twice she had asked him to show them to her. She often sat at a distance, with drooping head, and gazed at him. He did not care. It was Inge he loved, blonde, jolly Inge, who most assuredly despised him for his poetic effusions . . . he looked at her, looked at her narrow blue eyes full of fun and mockery, and felt an envious longing; to be shut away from her like this, to be forever strange – he felt it in his breast, like a heavy, burning weight.

'First couple *en avant*,' said Herr Knaak; and no words can tell how marvellously he pronounced the nasal. They were to practise the quadrille, and to Tonio Kröger's profound alarm he found himself in the same set with Inge Holm. He avoided her where he could, yet somehow was forever near her; kept his eyes away from her person and yet found his gaze ever on her. There she came, tripping up hand-in-hand with red-headed Ferdinand Matthiessen; she flung back her braid, drew a deep breath, and took her place opposite Tonio. Herr Heinzelmann, at the piano, laid bony hands upon the keys. Herr Knaak waved his arm, the quadrille began.

She moved to and fro before his eyes, forwards and back, pacing and swinging; he seemed to catch a fragrance from her hair or the folds of her thin white frock, and his eyes grew sadder and sadder. 'I love you, dear, sweet Inge,' he said to himself, and put into his words all the pain he felt to see her so intent upon the dance with not a thought of him. Some lines of an exquisite poem by Storm came into his mind: 'I would sleep, but thou must dance.' It seemed against all sense, and most depressing, that he must be dancing when he was in love. . . .

'First couple *en avant*,' said Herr Knaak; it was the next figure. '*Compliment! Moulinet des dames! Tour de main!*' and he swallowed the silent *e* in the '*de*', with quite indescribable ease and grace.

'Second couple *en avant!*' This was Tonio Kröger and his partner. '*Compliment!*' And Tonio Kröger bowed. '*Moulinet des dames!*' And Tonio Kröger, with bent head and gloomy brows, laid his hand on those of the four ladies, on Ingeborg Holm's hand, and danced the *moulinet*.

Roundabout rose a tittering and laughing. Herr Knaak took a ballet pose conventionally expressive of horror. 'Oh, dear! Oh, dear!' he cried. 'Stop! Stop! Kröger among the ladies! *En arrière*, Fräulein Kröger, step back, *fi donc!* Everybody else understood it but you. Shoo! Get out! Get away!' He drew out his yellow silk handkerchief and flapped Tonio Kröger back to his place.

Everyone laughed, the girls and the boys and the ladies beyond the portières; Herr Knaak had made something too utterly funny out of the little episode, it was as amusing as a play. But Herr Heinzelmann at the piano sat and waited, with a dry, business-like air, for a sign to go on; he was hardened against Herr Knaak's effects.

Then the quadrille went on. And the intermission followed. The parlourmaid came clinking in with a tray of wine-jelly glasses, the cook followed in her wake with a load of plum-cake. But Tonio Kröger stole away. He stole out into the corridor and stood there, his hands behind his back, in front of a window with the blind down. He never thought that one could not see through the blind and that it was absurd to stand there as though one were looking out.

For he was looking within, into himself, the theatre of so much pain and longing. Why, why was he here? Why was he not sitting by the window in his own room, reading Storm's *Immensee* and lifting his eyes to the twilight garden outside, where the old walnut tree moaned? That was the place for him! Others might dance, others bend their fresh and lively minds upon the pleasure in hand! . . . But no, no, after all, his place was here, where he could feel near Inge, even although he stood lonely and aloof, seeking to distinguish the warm notes of her voice amid the buzzing, clattering and laughter within. Oh, lovely Inge, blonde Inge of the narrow, laughing blue eyes! So lovely and laughing as you are one can only be if one does not read *Immensee* and never tries to write things like it. And that was just the tragedy!

Ah, she *must* come! She *must* notice where he had gone, must feel how he suffered! She must slip out to him, even pity must bring her, to lay her hand on his shoulder and say: 'Do come back to us, ah, don't be sad – I love you, Tonio.' He listened behind him and waited in frantic suspense. But not in the least. Such things did not happen on this earth.

Had she laughed at him too, like all the others? Yes, she had, however gladly he would have denied it for both their sakes. And yet it was only because he had been so taken up with her that he had danced the *moulinet des dames*. Suppose he had – what did that matter? Had not a magazine accepted a poem of his a little while ago – even though the magazine had failed before his poem could be printed? The day was coming when he would be famous, when they would print everything he wrote; and *then* he would see if that made any impression on Inge Holm! No, it would make no impression at all; that was just it. Magdalena Vermehren, who was always falling down in the dances, yes, she would be impressed. But never Ingeborg Holm, never blue-eyed, laughing Inge. So what was the good of it?

Tonio Kröger's heart contracted painfully at the thought. To feel stirring within you the wonderful and melancholy play of strange forces and to be aware that those others you yearn for are blithely inaccessible to all that moves you – what a pain is this! And yet! He stood there aloof and alone, staring hopelessly at a drawn blind and making, in his distraction, as though he could look out. But yet he was happy. For he lived. His heart was full; hotly and sadly it beat for thee, Ingeborg Holm, and his soul embraced thy blonde, simple, pert, commonplace little personality in blissful self-abnegation.

Often after that he stood thus, with burning cheeks, in lonely corners, whither the sound of the music, the tinkling of glasses and fragrance of flowers came but faintly, and tried to distinguish the ringing tones of thy voice amid the distant happy din; stood suffering for thee – and still was happy! Often it angered him to think that he might talk with Magdalena Vermehren, who always fell down in the dance. She understood him, she laughed or was serious in the right places; while Inge the fair, let him sit never so near her, seemed remote and estranged, his speech not being her speech. And still – he was happy. For happiness, he told himself, is not in being loved – which is a satisfaction of the vanity and mingled with disgust. Happiness is in loving and perhaps in snatching fugitive little approaches to the beloved object. And he took inward note of this thought, wrote it down in his mind; followed out all its implications and felt it to the depths of his soul.

'Faithfulness,' thought Tonio Kröger. 'Yes, I will be faithful, I will love thee, Ingeborg, as long as I live!' He said this in the honesty of his intentions. And yet a still small voice whispered misgivings in his ear: after all, he had forgotten Hans Hansen utterly, even though he saw him every day! And the hateful, the pitiable fact was that this still, small, rather spiteful voice was right: time passed and the day came when Tonio Kröger was no longer so unconditionally ready as once he had been to die for the lively Inge, because he felt in himself desires and powers to accomplish in his own way a host of wonderful things in this world.

And he circled with watchful eye the sacrificial altar, where flickered the pure, chaste flame of his love; knelt before it and tended and cherished it in every way, because he so wanted to be faithful. And in a little while, unobservably, without sensation or stir, it went out after all.

But Tonio Kröger still stood before the cold altar, full of regret and dismay at the fact that faithfulness was impossible upon this earth. Then he shrugged his shoulders and went his way.

He went the way that go he must, a little idly, a little irregularly, whistling to himself, gazing into space with his head on one side; and if he went wrong, it was because for some people there is no such thing as a right way. Asked what in the world he meant to become, he gave various answers, for he was used to say (and had even already written it) that he bore within himself the possibility of a thousand ways of life, together with the private conviction that they were all sheer impossibilities.

Even before he left the narrow streets of his native city, the threads that bound him to it had gently loosened. The old Kröger family gradually declined, and some people quite rightly considered Tonio Kröger's own existence and way of life as one of the signs of decay. His father's mother, the head of the family, had died, and not long after his own father followed, the tall, thoughtful, carefully dressed gentleman with the field-flower in his buttonhole. The great Kröger house, with all its stately tradition, came up for sale, and the firm was dissolved. Tonio's mother, his beautiful, fiery mother, who played the piano and mandolin so wonderfully and to whom nothing mattered at all, she married again after a year's time; married a musician, moreover, a virtuoso with an Italian name, and went away with him into remote blue distances. Tonio Kröger found this a little irregular, but who was he to call her to order, who wrote poetry himself and could not even give an answer when asked what he meant to do in life?

And so he left his native town and its tortuous, gabled streets with the damp wind whistling through them; left the fountain in the garden and the ancient walnut tree, familiar friends of his youth; left the sea too, that he loved so much, and felt no pain to go. For he was grown up and sensible and had come to realize how things stood with him; he looked down on the lowly and vulgar life he had led so long in these surroundings.

He surrendered utterly to the power that to him seemed the

highest on earth, to whose service he felt called, which promised him elevation and honours: the power of intellect, the power of the Word, that lords it with a smile over the unconscious and inarticulate. To this power he surrendered with all the passion of youth, and it rewarded him with all it had to give, taking from him inexorably, in return, all that it is wont to take.

It sharpened his eyes and made him see through the large words which puff out the bosoms of mankind; it opened for him men's souls and his own, made him clairvoyant, showed him the inwardness of the world and the ultimate behind men's words and deeds. And all that he saw could be put in two words: the comedy and the tragedy of life.

And then, with knowledge, its torment and its arrogance, came solitude; because he could not endure the blithe and innocent with their darkened understanding, while they in turn were troubled by the sign on his brow. But his love of the Word kept growing sweeter and sweeter, and his love of form; for he used to say (and had already said it in writing) that knowledge of the soul would unfailingly make us melancholy if the pleasures of expression did not keep us alert and of good cheer.

He lived in large cities and in the south, promising himself a luxuriant ripening of his art by southern suns; perhaps it was the blood of his mother's race that drew him thither. But his heart being dead and loveless, he fell into adventures of the flesh, descended into the depths of lust and searing sin, and suffered unspeakably thereby. It might have been his father in him, that tall, thoughtful, fastidiously dressed man with the wild flower in his buttonhole, that made him suffer so down there in the south; now and again he would feel a faint, yearning memory of a certain joy that was of the soul; once it had been his own, but now, in all his joys, he could not find it again.

Then he would be seized with disgust and hatred of the

senses; pant after purity and seemly peace, while still he breathed the air of art, the tepid, sweet air of permanent spring, heavy with fragrance where it breeds and brews and burgeons in the mysterious bliss of creation. So for all result he was flung to and fro forever between two crass extremes: between icy intellect and scorching sense, and what with his pangs of conscience led an exhausting life, rare, extraordinary, excessive, which at bottom he, Tonio Kröger, despised. 'What a labyrinth!' he sometimes thought. 'How could I possibly have got into all these fantastic adventures? As though I had a wagonful of travelling gypsies for my ancestors!'

But as his health suffered from these excesses, so his artistry was sharpened; it grew fastidious, precious, *raffiné*, morbidly sensitive in questions of tact and taste, rasped by the banal. His first appearance in print elicited much applause; there was joy among the elect, for it was a good and workmanlike performance, full of humour and acquaintance with pain. In no long time his name – the same by which his masters had reproached him, the same he had signed to his earliest verses on the walnut tree and the fountain and the sea, those syllables compact of the north and the south, that good middle-class name with the exotic twist to it – became a synonym for excellence; for the painful thoroughness of the experiences he had gone through, combined with a tenacious ambition and a persistent industry, joined battle with the irritable fastidiousness of his taste and under grinding torments issued in work of a quality quite uncommon.

He worked, not like a man who works that he may live; but as one who is bent on doing nothing but work; having no regard for himself as a human being but only as a creator; moving about grey and unobtrusive among his fellows like an actor without his make-up, who counts for nothing as soon as he stops representing something else. He worked withdrawn out of sight and sound of the small fry, for whom he felt nothing but contempt, because to them a talent was a social asset like another; who, whether they were poor or not, went about ostentatiously shabby or else flaunted startling cravats, all the time taking jolly good care to amuse themselves, to be artistic and charming without the smallest notion of the fact that good work only comes out under pressure of a bad life; that <u>he who lives does not work</u>; that one must die to life in order to be utterly a creator.

'Shall I disturb you?' asked Tonio Kröger on the threshold of the *atelier*. He held his hat in his hand and bowed with some ceremony, although Lisabeta Ivanovna was a good friend of his, to whom he told all his troubles.

'Mercy on you, Tonio Kröger! Don't be so formal,' answered she, with her lilting intonation. 'Everybody knows you were taught good manners in your nursery.' She transferred her brush to her left hand, that held the palette, reached him her right, and looked him in the face, smiling and shaking her head.

'Yes, but you are working,' he said. 'Let's see. Oh, you've been getting on,' and he looked at the colour-sketches leaning against chairs at both sides of the easel and from them to the large canvas covered with a square linen mesh, where the first patches of colour were beginning to appear among the confused and schematic lines of the charcoal sketch.

This was in Munich, in a back building in Schellingstrasse several storeys up. Beyond the wide window facing the north were blue sky, sunshine, birds twittering; the young sweet breath of spring streaming through an open pane mingled with the smells of paint and fixative. The afternoon light, bright golden, flooded the spacious emptiness of the atelier; it made no secret of the bad flooring or the rough table under the window, covered with little bottles, tubes, and brushes; it illumined the unframed studies on the unpapered walls, the torn silk screen that shut off a charmingly furnished little living-corner near the door; it shone upon the inchoate work on the easel, upon the artist and the poet there before it.

She was about the same age as himself – slightly past thirty. She sat there on a low stool, in her dark-blue apron, and leant her chin in her hand. Her brown hair, compactly dressed, already a little grey at the sides, was parted in the middle and waved over the temples, framing a sensitive, sympathetic, dark-skinned face, which was Slavic in its facial structure, with flat nose, strongly accentuated cheek-bones, and little bright black eyes. She sat there measuring her work with her head on one side and her eyes screwed up; her features were drawn with a look of misgiving, almost of vexation.

He stood beside her, his right hand on his hip, with the other furiously twirling his brown moustache. His dress, reserved in cut and a soothing shade of grey, was punctilious and dignified to the last degree. He was whistling softly to himself, in the way he had, and his slanting brows were gathered in a frown. The dark-brown hair was parted with severe correctness, but the laboured forehead beneath showed a nervous twitching, and the chiselled southern features were sharpened as though they had been gone over again with a graver's tool. And yet the mouth – how gently curved it was, the chin how softly formed! . . . After a little he drew his hand across his brow and eyes and turned away.

'I ought not to have come,' he said.

'And why not, Tonio Kröger?'

'I've just got up from my desk, Lisabeta, and inside my head it looks just the way it does on this canvas. A scaffolding, a faint first draft smeared with corrections and a few splotches of colour; yes, and I come up here and see the same thing. And the same conflict and contradiction in the air,' he went on, sniffing, 'that has been torturing me at home. It's extraordinary. If you are possessed by an idea, you find it expressed everywhere, you even *smell* it. Fixative and the breath of spring; art and – what? Don't say nature, Lisabeta, "nature" isn't exhausting. Ah, no, I ought to have gone for a walk, though it's doubtful if it would have made me feel better.

Five minutes ago, not far from here, I met a man I know, Adalbert, the novelist. "God damn the spring!" says he in the aggressive way he has. "It is and always has been the most ghastly time of the year. Can you get hold of a single sensible idea, Kröger? Can you sit still and work out even the smallest effect, when your blood tickles till it's positively indecent and you are teased by a whole host of irrelevant sensations that when you look at them turn out to be unworkable trash? For my part, I am going to a café. A café is neutral territory, the change of the seasons doesn't affect it; it represents, so to speak, the detached and elevated sphere of the literary man, in which one is only capable of refined ideas." And he went into the café . . . and perhaps I ought to have gone with him.'

Lisabeta was highly entertained.

'I like that, Tonio Kröger. That part about the indecent tickling is good. And he is right too, in a way, for spring is really not very conducive to work. But now listen. Spring or no spring, I will just finish this little place – work out this little effect, as your friend Adalbert would say. Then we'll go into the "salon" and have tea, and you can talk yourself out, for I can perfectly well see you are too full for utterance. Will you just compose yourself somewhere – on that chest, for instance, if you are not afraid for your aristocratic garments – –'

'Oh, leave my clothes alone, Lisabeta Ivanovna! Do you want me to go about in a ragged velveteen jacket or a red waistcoat? Every artist is as bohemian as the deuce inside! Let him at least wear proper clothes and behave outwardly like a respectable being. No. I am not too full for utterance,' he said as he watched her mixing her paints. 'I've told you, it is only that I have a problem and a conflict that sticks in my mind and disturbs me at my work. . . . Yes, what was it we were just saying? We were talking about Adalbert, the novelist, that stout and forthright man. "Spring is the most ghastly time of the year," says he, and goes into a café. A man has to know what he needs, eh? Well, you see he's not the only one; the spring makes me nervous, too; I get dazed with the trifling-ness and sacredness of the memories and feelings it evokes; only that I don't succeed in looking down on it; for the truth is it makes me ashamed; I quail before its sheer naturalness and triumphant youth. And I don't know whether I should envy Adalbert or despise him for his ignorance. . . .

'Yes, it is true; spring is a bad time for work; and why? Because we are feeling too much. Nobody but a beginner imagines that he who creates must feel. Every real and genuine artist smiles at such naïve blunders as that. A melancholy enough smile, perhaps, but still a smile. For what an artist talks about is never the main point; it is the raw material, in and for itself indifferent, out of which, with bland and serene mastery, he creates the work of art. If you care too much about what you have to say, if your heart is too much in it, you can be pretty sure of making a mess. You get pathetic, you wax sentimental; something dull and doddering, without roots or outlines, with no sense of humour – something tiresome and banal grows under your hand, and you get nothing out of it but apathy in your audience and disappointment and misery in yourself. For so it is, Lisabeta; feeling, warm, heartfelt feeling, is always banal and futile; only the irritations and icy ecstasies of the artist's corrupted nervous system are artis-tic. The artist must be unhuman, extra-human; he must stand in a queer aloof relationship to our humanity; only so is he in a position, I ought to say only so would he be tempted, to represent it, to present it, to portray it to good effect. The very gift of style of form and expression, is nothing else than this cool and fastidious attitude towards humanity; you might say there has to be this impoverishment and devastation as a preliminary condition. For sound natural feeling, say what you like, has no taste. It is all up with the artist as soon as he becomes a man and begins to feel. Adalbert knows that; that's why he be-took himself to the café, the neutral territory – God help him!'

'Yes, God help him, Batuschka,' said Lisabeta, as she washed her hands in a tin basin. 'You don't need to follow his example.'

'No, Lisabeta, I am not going to; and the only reason is that I am now and again in a position to feel a little ashamed of the springtime of my art. You see sometimes I get letters from strangers, full of praise and thanks and admiration from people whose feelings I have touched. I read them and feel touched myself at these warm if ungainly emotions I have called up; a sort of pity steals over me at this naïve enthusiasm; and I positively blush at the thought of how these good people would freeze up if they were to get a look behind the scenes. What they, in their innocence, cannot comprehend is that a properly constituted, healthy, decent man never writes, acts, or composes – all of which does not hinder me from using his admiration for my genius to goad myself on; nor from taking it in deadly earnest and aping the airs of a great man. Oh, don't talk to me, Lisabeta. I tell you I am sick to death of depicting humanity without having any part or lot in it. . . . Is an artist a male, anyhow? Ask the females! It seems to me we artists are all of us something like those unsexed papal singers . . . we sing like angels; but – –'

'Shame on you, Tonio Kröger. But come to tea. The water is just on the boil, and here are some *papyros*. You were talking about singing soprano, do go on. But really you ought to be ashamed of yourself. If I did not know your passionate devotion to your calling and how proud you are of it – –'

'Don't talk about "calling", Lisabeta Ivanovna. Literature is not a calling, it is a curse, believe me! When does one begin to feel the curse? Early, horribly early. At a time when one ought by rights still to be living in peace and harmony with God and the world. It begins by your feeling yourself set apart, in a curious sort of opposition to the nice, regular people; there is a gulf of ironic sensibility, of knowledge, scepticism, disagreement, between you and the others; it grows deeper and deeper, you realize that you are alone; and from then on any *rapprochement* is simply hopeless! What a fate! That is, if you still have enough heart, enough warmth of affections, to feel how frightful it is! . . . Your self-consciousness is kindled, because you among thousands feel the sign on your brow and know that everyone else sees it. I once knew an actor, a man of genius, who had to struggle with a morbid self-consciousness and instability. When he had no rôle to play, nothing to represent, this man, consummate artist but impoverished human being, was overcome by an exaggerated consciousness of his ego. A genuine artist – not one who has taken up art as a profession like another, but artist foreordained and damned – you can pick out, without boasting very sharp perceptions, out of a group of men. The sense of being set apart and not belonging, of being known and observed, something both regal and incongruous shows in his face. You might see something of the same sort on the features of a prince walking through a crowd in ordinary clothes. But no civilian clothes are any good here, Lisabeta. You can disguise yourself, you can dress up like an attaché or a lieutenant of the guard on leave; you hardly need to give a glance or speak a word before everyone knows you are not a human being, but something else: something queer, different, inimical.

'But what is it, to be an artist? Nothing shows up the general human dislike of thinking, and man's innate craving to be comfortable, better than his attitude to this question. When these worthy people are affected by a work of art, they say humbly that that sort of thing is a 'gift'. And because in their innocence they assume that beautiful and uplifting results must have beautiful and and uplifting causes, they never dream that the "gift" in question is a very dubious affair and rests upon extremely sinister foundations. Everybody knows that artists are "sensitive" and easily wounded; just as everybody knows that ordinary people, with a normal bump of self-confidence, are not. Now you see, Lisabeta, I cherish at the bottom of my soul all the scorn and suspicion of the artist gentry – translated into terms of the intellectual – that my upright old forbears there on the Baltic would have felt for any juggler or mountebank that entered their houses. Listen to this. I know a banker, a grey-haired business man, who has a gift for writing stories. He employs this gift in his idle hours, and some of his stories are of the first rank. But despite – I say despite – this excellent gift his withers are by no means unwrung: on the contrary, he has had to serve a prison sentence, on anything but trifling grounds. Yes, it was actually first *in prison* that he became conscious of his gift, and his experiences as a convict are the main theme in all his works. One might be rash enough to conclude that a man has to be at home in some kind of jail in order to become a poet. But can you escape the suspicion that the source and essence of his being an artist had less to do with his life in prison than they had with the reasons that *brought him there*? A banker who writes – that is a rarity, isn't it? But a banker who isn't a criminal, who is irreproachably respectable, and yet writes – he doesn't exist. Yes, you are laughing, and yet I am more than half serious. No problem, none in the world, is more tormenting than this of the artist and his human aspect. Take the most miraculous case of all, take the most typical and therefore the most powerful of artists, take such a morbid and profoundly equivocal work as *Tristan and Isolde*, and look at the effect it has on a healthy young man of thoroughly normal feelings. Exaltation, encouragement, warm, downright enthusiasm, perhaps incitement to "artistic" creation of his own. Poor young dilettante! In us artists it looks fundamentally different from what he wots of, with his "warm heart" and "honest enthusiasm". I've seen women and youths go mad over artists . . . and I *knew* about them . . . ! The origin, the accompanying phenomena, and the conditions of the artist life –

good Lord, what I haven't observed about them, over and over!'

'Observed, Tonio Kröger? If I may ask, only "observed"?'

He was silent, knitting his oblique brown brows and whistling softly to himself.

'Let me have your cup, Tonio. The tea is weak. And take another cigarette. Now, you perfectly know that you are looking at things as they do not necessarily have to be looked at. . . .'

'That is Horatio's answer, dear Lisabeta. "'Twere to consider too curiously, to consider so."'

'I mean, Tonio Kröger, that one can consider them just exactly as well from another side. I am only a silly painting female, and if I can contradict you at all, if I can defend your own profession a little against you, it is not by saying anything new, but simply by reminding you of some things you very well know yourself: of the purifying and healing influence of letters, the subduing of the passions by knowledge and eloquence; literature as the guide to understanding, forgiveness and love, the redeeming power of the word, literary art as the noblest manifestation of the human mind, the poet as the most highly developed of human beings, the poet as saint. Is it to consider things not curiously enough, to consider them so?'

'You may talk like that, Lisabeta Ivanovna, you have a perfect right. And with reference to Russian literature, and the works of your poets, one can really worship them; they really come close to being that elevated literature you are talking about. But I am not ignoring your objections, they are part of the things I have in my mind to-day. . . . Look at me, Lisabeta. I don't look any too cheerful, do I? A little old and tired and pinched, eh? Well, now to come back to the "knowledge". Can't you imagine a man, born orthodox, mild-mannered, well-meaning, a bit sentimental, just simply over-stimulated by his psychological clairvoyance, and going to the dogs? Not to let the sadness of the world unman you; to read, mark, learn, and put to account even the most torturing things and to be of perpetual good cheer, in the sublime consciousness of moral superiority over the horrible invention of existence – yes, thank you! But despite all the joys of expression once in a while the thing gets on your nerves. "*Tout comprendre c'est tout pardonner.*" I don't know about that. There is something I call being sick of knowledge, Lisabeta: when it is enough for you to see through a thing in order to be sick to death of it, and not in the least in a forgiving mood. Such was the case of Hamlet the Dane, that typical literary man. He knew what it meant to be called to knowledge without being born to it. To see things clear, if even through your tears, to recognize, notice, observe – and have to put it all down with a smile, at the very moment when hands are clinging, and lips meeting, and the human gaze is blinded with feeling – it is infamous, Lisabeta, it is indecent, outrageous – but what good does it do to be outraged?

'Then another and no less charming side of the thing, of course, is your ennui, your indifferent and ironic attitude towards truth. It is a fact that there is no society in the world so dumb and hopeless as a circle of literary people who are hounded to death as it is. All knowledge is old and tedious to them. Utter some truth that it gave you considerable youthful joy to conquer and possess – and they will all chortle at you for your *naïveté*. Oh, yes, Lisabeta, literature is a wearing job. In human society, I do assure you, a reserved and sceptical man can be taken for stupid, whereas he is really only arrogant and perhaps lacks courage. So much for "knowledge". Now for the "Word". It isn't so much a matter of the "redeeming power" as it is of putting your emotions on ice and serving them up chilled! Honestly, don't you think there's a good deal of cool cheek in the prompt and superficial way a writer can get rid of his feelings by turning them into literature? If your heart is too full, if you are overpowered with the emotions of some sweet or exalted moment – nothing simpler! Go to the literary man, he will put it all straight for you *instanter*. He will analyse and formulate your affair, label it and express it and discuss it and polish it off and make you indifferent to it for time and eternity – and not charge you a farthing. You will go home quite relieved, cooled off, enlightened; and wonder what it was all about and why you were so mightily moved. And will you seriously enter the lists in behalf of this vain and frigid charlatan? What is uttered, so runs this *credo*, is finished and done with. If the whole world could be expressed, it would be saved, finished and done. . . . Well and good. But I am not a nihilist – –'

'You are not a – –' said Lisabeta. . . . She was lifting a tea-spoonful of tea to her mouth and paused in the act to stare at him.

'Come, come, Lisabeta, what's the matter? I say I am not a nihilist, with respect, that is, to lively feeling. You see the literary man does not understand that life may go on living, unashamed, even after it has been expressed and therewith finished. No matter how much it has been redeemed by becoming literature, it keeps right on sinning – for all action is sin in the mind's eye – –

'I'm nearly done, Lisabeta.   Please listen. I love life – this is an admission. I present it to you, you may have it. I have never made it to anyone else. People say – people have even written and printed – that I hate life, or fear or despise or abominate it. I liked to hear this, it has always flattered me; but that does not make it true. I love life. You smile; and I know why, Lisabeta. But I implore you not to take what I am saying for literature. Don't think of Caesar Borgia or any drunken philosophy that has him for a standard-bearer. He is nothing to me, your Caesar Borgia. I have no opinion of him, and I shall never comprehend how one can honour the extraordinary and daemonic as an ideal. No, life as the eternal antinomy of mind and art does not represent itself to us as a

vision of savage greatness and ruthless beauty; we who are
set apart and different do not conceive it as, like us, unusual;
it is the normal, respectable, and admirable that is the kingdom
of our longing: life, in all its seductive banality! That man is
very far from being an artist, my dear, whose last and deepest
enthusiasm is the *raffiné*, the eccentric and satanic; who does
not know a longing for the innocent, the simple, and the
living, for a little friendship, devotion, familiar human happiness – the gnawing, surreptitious hankering, Lisabeta, for
the bliss of the commonplace. . . .

'A genuine human friend. Believe me, I should be proud
and happy to possess a friend among men. But up to now all
the friends I have had have been daemons, kobolds, impious
monsters, and spectres dumb with excess of knowledge – that
is to say, literary men.

'I may be standing upon some platform, in some hall in
front of people who have come to listen to me. And I find
myself looking round among my hearers, I catch myself
secretly peering about the auditorium, and all the while I am
thinking who it is that has come here to listen to me, whose
grateful applause is in my ears, with whom my art is making
me one. . . . I do not find what I seek, Lisabeta, I find the
herd. The same old community, the same old gathering of
early Christians, so to speak: people with fine souls in uncouth bodies, people who are always falling down in the
dance, if you know what I mean; the kind to whom poetry
serves as a sort of mild revenge on life. Always and only the
poor and suffering, never any of the others, the blue-eyed
ones, Lisabeta – they do not need mind. . . .

'And, after all, would it not be a lamentable lack of logic to
want it otherwise? It is against all sense to love life and yet
bend all the powers you have to draw it over to your own
side, to the side of finesse and melancholy and the whole sickly
aristocracy of letters. The kingdom of art increases and that
of health and innocence declines on this earth. What there is

left of it ought to be carefully preserved; one ought not to tempt people to read poetry who would much rather read books about the instantaneous photography of horses.

'For, after all, what more pitiable sight is there than life led astray by art? We artists have a consummate contempt for the dilettante, the man who is leading a living life and yet thinks he can be an artist too if he gets the chance. I am speaking from personal experience, I do assure you. Suppose I am in a company in a good house, with eating and drinking going on, and plenty of conversation and good feeling; I am glad and grateful to be able to lose myself among good regular people for a while. Then all of a sudden – I am thinking of something that actually happened – an officer gets up, a lieutenant, a stout, good-looking chap, whom I could never have believed guilty of any conduct unbecoming his uniform, and actually in good set terms asks the company's permission to read some verses of his own composition. Everybody looks disconcerted, they laugh and tell him to go on, and he takes them at their word and reads from a sheet of paper he has up to now been hiding in his coat-tail pocket – something about love and music, as deeply felt as it is inept. But I ask you: a lieutenant! A man of the world! He surely did not need to. . . . Well, the inevitable result is long faces, silence, a little artificial applause, everybody thoroughly uncomfortable. The first sensation I am conscious of is guilt – I feel partly responsible for the disturbance this rash youth has brought upon the company; and no wonder, for I, as a member of the same guild, am a target for some of the unfriendly glances. But next minute I realize something else: this man for whom just now I felt the greatest respect has suddenly sunk in my eyes. I feel a benevolent pity. Along with some other brave and good-natured gentlemen I go up and speak to him. "Congratulations, Herr Lieutenant," I say, "that is a very pretty talent you have. It was charming." And I am within an ace of clapping him on the shoulder. But is that the way one is supposed to feel towards a lieutenant –

benevolent? . . . It was his own fault. There he stood, suffering embarrassment for the mistake of thinking that one may pluck a single leaf from the laurel tree of art without paying for it with his life. No, there I go with my colleague, the convict banker – but don't you find, Lisabeta, that I have quite a Hamlet-like flow of oratory to-day?'

'Are you done, Tonio Kröger?'

'No. But there won't be any more.'

'And quite enough too. Are you expecting a reply?'

'Have you one ready?'

'I should say. I have listened to you faithfully, Tonio, from beginning to end, and I will give you the answer to everything you have said this afternoon and the solution of the problem that has been upsetting you. Now: the solution is that you, as you sit there, are, quite simply, a bourgeois.'

'Am I?' he asked a little crestfallen.

'Yes; that hits you hard, it must. So I will soften the judgement just a little. You are a bourgeois on the wrong path, a bourgeois *manqué*.'

Silence. Then he got up resolutely and took his hat and stick.

'Thank you, Lisabeta Ivanovna; now I can go home in peace. I am expressed.'

Towards autumn Tonio Kröger said to Lisabeta Ivanovna: 'Well, Lisabeta, I think I'll be off. I need a change of air. I must get away, out into the open.'

'Well, well, well, little Father! Does it please your Highness to go down to Italy again?'

'Oh, get along with your Italy, Lisabeta. I'm fed up with Italy, I spew it out of my mouth. It's a long time since I imagined I could belong down there. Art, eh? Blue-velvet sky, ardent wine, the sweets of sensuality. In short, I don't want it – I decline with thanks. The whole *bellezza* business makes me nervous. All those frightfully animated people down there with their black animal-like eyes; I don't like them either.

These Romance peoples have no soul in their eyes. No, I'm going to take a trip to Denmark.'

'To Denmark?'

'Yes. I'm quite sanguine of the results. I happen never to have been there, though I lived all my youth so close to it. Still I have always known and loved the country. I suppose I must have this northern tendency from my father, for my mother was really more for the *bellezza*, in so far, that is, as she cared very much one way or the other. But just take the books that are written up there, that clean, meaty whimsical Scandinavian literature, Lisabeta, there's nothing like it, I love it. Or take the Scandinavian meals, those incomparable meals, which can only be digested in strong sea air (I don't know whether I can digest them in any sort of air); I know them from my home too, because we ate that way up there. Take even the names, the given names that people rejoice in up north; we have a good many of them in my part of the country too: Ingeborg, for instance, isn't it the purest poetry – like a harp-tone? And then the sea – up there it's the Baltic! . . . In a word, I am going, Lisabeta. I want to see the Baltic again and read the books and hear the names on their native heath; I want to stand on the terrace at Kronberg, where the ghost appeared to Hamlet, bringing despair and death to that poor, noble-souled youth. . . .'

'How are you going, Tonio, if I may ask? What route are you taking?'

'The usual one,' he said, shrugging his shoulders, and blushed perceptibly. 'Yes, I shall touch my – my point of departure, Lisabeta, after thirteen years, and that may turn out rather funny.'

She smiled.

'That is what I wanted to hear, Tonio Kröger. Well, be off, then, in God's name. Be sure to write to me, do you hear? I shall expect a letter full of your experiences in – Denmark.'

And Tonio Kröger travelled north. He travelled in comfort (for he was wont to say that anyone who suffered inwardly more than other people had a right to a little outward ease); and he did not stay until the towers of the little town he had left rose up in the grey air. Among them he made a short and singular stay.

The dreary afternoon was merging into evening when the train pulled into the narrow, reeking shed, so marvellously familiar. The volumes of thick smoke rolled up to the dirty glass roof and wreathed to and fro there in long tatters, just as they had, long ago, on the day when Tonio Kröger, with nothing but derision in his heart, had left his native town. – He arranged to have his luggage sent to his hotel and walked out of the station.

There were the cabs, those enormously high, enormously wide black cabs drawn by two horses, standing in a rank. He did not take one, he only looked at them, as he looked at everything: the narrow gables, and the pointed towers peering above the roofs close at hand; the plump, fair, easy-going populace, with their broad yet rapid speech. And a nervous laugh mounted in him, mysteriously akin to a sob. – He walked on, slowly, with the damp wind constantly in his face, across the bridge, with the mythological statues on the railings and some distance along the harbour.

Good Lord, how tiny and close it all seemed! The comical little gabled streets were climbing up just as of yore from the port to the town! And on the ruffled waters the smoke-stacks and masts of the ships dipped gently in the wind and twilight. Should he go up that next street, leading, he knew, to a certain house? No, to-morrow. He was too sleepy. His head was heavy from the journey, and slow, vague trains of thought passed through his mind.

Sometimes in the past thirteen years, when he was suffering from indigestion, he had dreamed of being back home in the echoing old house in the steep, narrow street. His father had been there too, and reproached him bitterly for his dissolute manner of life, and this, each time, he had found quite as it should be. And now the present refused to distinguish itself in any way from one of those tantalizing dream-fabrications in which the dreamer asks himself if this be delusion or reality and is driven to decide for the latter, only to wake up after all in the end. . . . He paced through the half-empty streets with his head inclined against the wind, moving as though in his sleep in the direction of the hotel, the first hotel in the town, where he meant to sleep. A bow-legged man, with a pole at the end of which burned a tiny fire, walked before him with a rolling, seafaring gait and lighted the gas-lamps.

What was at the bottom of this? What was it burning darkly beneath the ashes of his fatigue, refusing to burst out into a clear blaze? Hush, hush, only no talk. Only don't make words! He would have liked to go on so, for a long time, in the wind, through the dusky, dreamily familiar streets – but everything was so little and close together here. You reached your goal at once.

In the upper town there were arc-lamps, just lighted. There was the hotel with the two black lions in front of it; he had been afraid of them as a child. And there they were, still looking at each other as though they were about to sneeze; only they seemed to have grown much smaller. Tonio Kröger passed between them into the hotel.

As he came on foot, he was received with no great ceremony. There was a porter, and a lordly gentleman dressed in black, to do the honours; the latter, shoving back his cuffs with his little fingers, measured him from the crown of his head to the soles of his boots, obviously with intent to place him, to assign him to his proper category socially and hierarchically speaking and then mete out the suitable degree of courtesy. He seemed not to come to any clear decision and compromised on a moderate display of politeness. A mild-mannered waiter with yellow-white side-whiskers, in a dress suit shiny with age, and rosettes on his soundless shoes, led him up two flights into a clean old room furnished in patriarchal style. Its windows gave on a twilit view of courts and gables, very medieval and picturesque, with the fantastic bulk of the old church close by. Tonio Kröger stood awhile before this window; then he sat down on the wide sofa, crossed his arms, drew down his brows and whistled to himself.

Lights were brought and his luggage came up. The mild-mannered waiter laid the hotel register on the table, and Tonio Kröger, his head on one side, scrawled something on it that might be taken for a name, a station, and a place of origin. Then he ordered supper and went on gazing into space from his sofa-corner. When it stood before him he let it wait long untouched, then took a few bites and walked up and down an hour in his room, stopping from time to time and closing his eyes. Then he very slowly undressed and went to bed. He slept long and had curiously confused and ardent dreams.

It was broad day when he woke. Hastily he recalled where he was and got up to draw the curtains; the pale-blue sky, already with a hint of autumn, was streaked with frayed and tattered cloud; still, above his native city the sun was shining.

He spent more care than usual upon his toilette, washed and shaved and made himself fresh and immaculate as though about to call upon some smart family where a well-dressed and flawless appearance was *de rigueur;* and while occupied in this wise he listened to the anxious beating of his heart.

How bright it was outside! He would have liked better a twilight air like yesterday's, instead of passing through the streets in the broad sunlight, under everybody's eye. Would he meet people he knew, be stopped and questioned and have to submit to be asked how he had spent the last thirteen years? No, thank goodness, he was known to nobody here; even if anybody remembered him, it was unlikely he would be recognized – for certainly he had changed in the meantime! He surveyed himself in the glass and felt a sudden sense of security behind his mask, behind his work-worn face, that was older than his years. . . . He sent for breakfast, and after that he went out; he passed under the disdainful eye of the porter and the gentleman in black, through the vestibule and between the two lions, and so into the street.

Where was he going? He scarcely knew. It was the same as yesterday. Hardly was he in the midst of this long-familiar scene, this stately conglomeration of gables, turrets, arcades, and fountains, hardly did he feel once more the wind in his face, that strong current wafting a faint and pungent aroma from far-off dreams, than the same mistiness laid itself like a veil about his senses. . . . The muscles of his face relaxed, and he looked at men and things with a look grown suddenly calm. Perhaps right there, on that street corner, he might wake up after all. . . .

Where was he going? It seemed to him the direction he took had a connexion with his sad and strangely rueful dreams of the night. . . . He went to Market Square, under the vaulted arches of the Rathaus, where the butchers were weighing out their wares red-handed, where the tall old Gothic fountain stood with its manifold spires. He paused in front of a house, a plain narrow building, like many another, with a fretted baroque gable; stood there lost in contemplation. He read the plate on the door, his eyes rested a little while on each of the windows. Then slowly he turned away.

Where did he go? Towards home. But he took a round-about way outside the walls – for he had plenty of time. He went over the Millwall and over the Holstenwall, clutching his hat, for the wind was rushing and moaning through the trees. He left the wall near the station, where he saw a train puffing busily past, idly counted the coaches, and looked after the man who sat perched upon the last. In the Lindenplatz he stopped at one of the pretty villas, peered long into the garden and up at the windows, lastly conceived the idea of swinging the gate to and fro upon its hinges till it creaked. Then he looked awhile at his moist, rust-stained hand and went on, went through the squat old gate, along the harbour, and up the steep, windy street to his parents' house.

It stood aloof from its neighbours, its gable towering above them; grey and sombre, as it had stood these three hundred years; and Tonio Kröger read the pious, half-illegible motto above the entrance. Then he drew a long breath and went in.

His heart gave a throb of fear, lest his father might come out of one of the doors on the ground floor, in his office coat, with the pen behind his ear, and take him to task for his excesses. He would have found the reproach quite in order; but he got past unchidden. The inner door was ajar, which appeared to him reprehensible though at the same time he felt as one does in certain broken dreams, where obstacles melt away of themselves, and one presses onward in marvellous favour with fortune. The wide entry, paved with great square flags, echoed to his tread. Opposite the silent kitchen was the curious projecting structure, of rough boards, but cleanly varnished, that had been the servants' quarters. It was quite high up and could only be reached by a sort of ladder from the entry. But the great cupboards and carven presses were gone. The son of the house climbed the majestic staircase, with his hand on the white-enamelled, fret-work balustrade. At each step he lifted his hand, and put it down again with the next as though testing whether he could call back his ancient familiarity with the stout old railing. . . . But at the landing of the entresol he stopped. For on the entrance door was a white plate; and on it in black letters he read: 'Public Library'.

'Public Library?' thought Tonio Kröger. What were either literature or the public doing here? He knocked . . . heard a 'Come in', and obeying it with gloomy suspense gazed upon a scene of most unhappy alteration.

The storey was three rooms deep, and all the doors stood open. The walls were covered nearly all the way up with long rows of books in uniform bindings, standing in dark-coloured bookcases. In each room a poor creature of a man sat writing behind a sort of counter. The farthest two just turned their heads, but the nearest got up in haste and, leaning with both hands on the table, stuck out his head, pursed his lips, lifted his brows, and looked at the visitor with eagerly blinking eyes.

'I beg pardon,' said Tonio Kröger without turning his eyes from the book-shelves. 'I am a stranger here, seeing the sights. So this is your Public Library? May I examine your collection a little?'

'Certainly, with pleasure,' said the official, blinking still more violently. 'It is open to everybody. . . . Pray look about you. Should you care for a catalogue?'

'No, thanks,' answered Tonio Kröger, 'I shall soon find my way about.' And he began to move slowly along the walls, with the appearance of studying the rows of books. After a while he took down a volume, opened it, and posted himself at the window.

This was the breakfast-room. They had eaten here in the morning instead of in the big dining-room upstairs, with its white statues of gods and goddesses standing out against the blue walls. . . . Beyond there had been a bedroom, where his father's mother had died – only after a long struggle, old as she was, for she had been of a pleasure-loving nature and clung to life. And his father too had drawn his last breath in the same room: that tall, correct, slightly melancholy and pensive gentleman with the wild flower in his buttonhole. . . . Tonio had sat at the foot of his death-bed, quite given over to unutterable feelings of love and grief. His mother had knelt at the bedside, his lovely, fiery mother, dissolved in hot tears; and after that she had withdrawn with her artist into the far blue south. . . . And beyond still, the small third room, likewise full of books and presided over by a shabby man – that had been for years on end his own. Thither he had come after

school and a walk – like to-day's; against that wall his table
had stood with the drawer where he had kept his first clumsy
heart-felt attempts at verse. . . . The walnut tree . . . a pang
went through him. He gave a sidewise glance out at the window. The garden lay desolate, but there stood the old walnut
tree where it used to stand, groaning and creaking heavily
in the wind. And Tonio Kröger let his gaze fall upon the book
he had in his hands, an excellent piece of work, and very
familiar. He followed the black lines of print, the paragraphs,
the flow of words that flowed with so much art, mounting in
the ardour of creation to a certain climax and effect and then
as artfully breaking off. . . .

'Yes, that was well done,' he said; put back the book and
turned away. Then he saw that the functionary still stood bolt-
upright, blinking with a mingled expression of zeal and misgiving.

'A capital collection, I see,' said Tonio Kröger. 'I have
already quite a good idea of it. Much obliged to you. Good-
bye.' He went out; but it was a poor exit, and he felt sure
the official would stand there perturbed and blinking for
several minutes.

He felt no desire for further researches. He had been home.
Strangers were living upstairs in the large rooms behind the
pillared hall; the top of the stairs was shut off by a glass door
which used not to be there, and on the door was a plate. He
went away, down the steps, across the echoing corridor, and
left his parental home. He sought a restaurant, sat down in a
corner, and brooded over a heavy, greasy meal. Then he
returned to his hotel.

'I am leaving,' he said to the fine gentleman in black. 'This
afternoon.' And he asked for his bill, and for a carriage to take
him down to the harbour where he should take the boat for
Copenhagen. Then he went up to his room and sat there stiff
and still, with his cheek on his hand, looking down on the
table before him with absent eyes. Later he paid his bill and

packed his things. At the appointed hour the carriage was announced and Tonio Kröger went down in travel array.

At the foot of the stairs the gentleman in black was waiting. 'Beg pardon,' he said, shoving back his cuffs with his little fingers. . . . 'Beg pardon, but we must detain you just a moment. Herr Seehaase, the proprietor, would like to exchange two words with you. A matter of form. . . . He is back there. . . . If you will have the goodness to step this way. . . . It is only Herr Seehaase, the proprietor.'

And he ushered Tonio Kröger into the background of the vestibule. . . . There, in fact, stood Herr Seehaase. Tonio Kröger recognized him from old time. He was small, fat, and bow-legged. His shaven side-whisker was white, but he wore the same old low-cut dress coat and little velvet cap embroidered in green. He was not alone. Beside him, at a little high desk fastened into the wall, stood a policeman in a helmet, his gloved right hand resting on a document in coloured inks; he turned towards Tonio Kröger with his honest, soldierly face as though he expected Tonio to sink into the earth at his glance.

Tonio Kröger looked at the two and confined himself to waiting.

'You came from Munich?' the policeman asked at length in a heavy, good-natured voice.

Tonio Kröger said he had.

'You are going to Copenhagen?'

'Yes, I am on the way to a Danish seashore resort.'

'Seashore resort? Well, you must produce your papers,' said the policeman. He uttered the last word with great satisfaction.

'Papers . . . ?' He had no papers. He drew out his pocket-book and looked into it; but aside from notes there was nothing there but some proof-sheets of a story which he had taken along to finish reading. He hated relations with officials and had never got himself a passport. . . .

'I am sorry,' he said, 'but I don't travel with papers.'

'Ah!' said the policeman. 'And what might be your name?'

Tonio replied.

'Is that a fact?' asked the policeman, suddenly erect, and expanding his nostrils as wide as he could. . . .

'Yes, that is a fact,' answered Tonio Kröger.

'And what are you, anyhow?'

Tonio Kröger gulped and gave the name of his trade in a firm voice. Herr Seehaase lifted his head and looked him curiously in the face.

'H'm,' said the policeman. 'And you give out that you are not identical with an individdle named' – he said 'individdle' and then, referring to his document in coloured inks, spelled out an involved, fantastic name which mingled all the sounds of all the races – Tonio Kröger forgot it next minute – 'of unknown parentage and unspecified means,' he went on, 'wanted by the Munich police for various shady transactions, and probably in flight towards Denmark?'

'Yes, I give out all that, and more,' said Tonio Kröger, wriggling his shoulders. The gesture made a certain impression.

'What? Oh, yes, of course,' said the policeman. 'You say you can't show any papers – –'

Herr Seehaase threw himself into the breach.

'It is only a formality,' he said pacifically, 'nothing else. You must bear in mind the official is only doing his duty. If you could only identify yourself somehow – some document . . .'

They were all silent. Should he make an end of the business by revealing to Herr Seehaase that he was no swindler without specified means, no gypsy in a green wagon, but the son of the late Consul Kröger, a member of the Kröger family? No, he felt no desire to do that. After all, were not these guardians of civic order within their right? He even agreed with them – up to a point. He shrugged his shoulders and kept quiet.

'What have you got, then?' asked the policeman. 'In your portfoly, I mean?'

'Here? Nothing. Just a proof-sheet,' answered Tonio Kröger.

'Proof-sheet? What's that? Let's see it.'

And Tonio Kröger handed over his work. The policeman spread it out on the shelf and began reading. Herr Seehaase drew up and shared it with him. Tonio Kröger looked over their shoulders to see what they read. It was a good moment, a little effect he had worked out to a perfection. He had a sense of self-satisfaction.

'You see,' he said, 'there is my name. I wrote it, and it is going to be published, you understand.'

'All right, that will answer,' said Herr Seehaase with decision, gathered up the sheets and gave them back. 'That will have to answer, Peterson,' he repeated crisply, shutting his eyes and shaking his head as though to see and hear no more. 'We must not keep the gentleman any longer. The carriage is waiting. I implore you to pardon the little inconvenience, sir. The officer has only done his duty, but I told him at once he was on the wrong track. . . .'

'Indeed!' thought Tonio Kröger.

The officer seemed still to have his doubts; he muttered something else about individdle and document. But Herr Seehaase, overflowing with regrets, led his guest through the vestibule, accompanied him past the two lions to the carriage, and himself, with many respectful bows, closed the door upon him. And then the funny, high, wide old cab rolled and rattled and bumped down the steep, narrow street to the quay.

And such was the manner of Tonio Kröger's visit to his ancestral home.

*

Night fell and the moon swam up with silver gleam as Tonio Kröger's boat reached the open sea. He stood at the prow wrapped in his cloak against a mounting wind, and looked beneath into the dark going and coming of the waves as they hovered and swayed and came on, to meet with a clap and shoot erratically away in a bright gush of foam.

He was lulled in a mood of still enchantment. The episode at the hotel, their wanting to arrest him for a swindler in his own home, had cast him down a little, even although he found it quite in order – in a certain way. But after he came on board he had watched, as he used to do as a boy with his father, the lading of goods into the deep bowels of the boat, amid shouts of mingled Danish and Plattdeutsch; not only boxes and bales, but also a Bengal tiger and a polar bear were lowered in cages with stout iron bars. They had probably come from Hamburg and were destined for a Danish menagerie. He had enjoyed these distractions. And as the boat glided along between flat river-banks he quite forgot Officer Petersen's inquisition; while all the rest – his sweet, sad, rueful dreams of the night before, the walk he had taken, the walnut tree – had welled up again in his soul. The sea opened out and he saw in the distance the beach where he as a lad had been let listen to the ocean's summer dreams; saw the flashing of the lighthouse tower and the lights of the Kurhaus where he and his parents had lived. . . . The Baltic! He bent his head to the strong salt wind; it came sweeping on, it enfolded him, made him faintly giddy and a little deaf; and in that mild confusion of the senses all memory of evil, of anguish and error, effort and exertion of the will, sank away into joyous oblivion and were gone. The roaring, foaming, flapping, and slapping all about him came to his ears like the groan and rustle of an old walnut tree, the creaking of a garden gate. . . . More and more the darkness came on.

'The stars! Oh, by the Lord, look at the stars!' a voice suddenly said, with a heavy sing-song accent that seemed to come out of the inside of a tun. He recognized it. It belonged to a young man with red-blond hair who had been Tonio Kröger's neighbour at dinner in the salon. His dress was very simple, his eyes were red, and he had the moist and chilly look of a person who has just bathed. With nervous and self-conscious movements he had taken unto himself an astonishing quantity of lobster omelet. Now he leaned on the rail beside Tonio Kröger and looked up at the skies, holding his chin between thumb and forefinger. Beyond a doubt he was in one of those rare and festal and edifying moods that cause the barriers between man and man to fall; when the heart opens even to the stranger, and the mouth utters that which otherwise it would blush to speak. . . .

'Look, by dear sir, just look at the stars. There they stahd and glitter; by goodness, the whole sky is full of theb! And I ask you, when you stahd ahd look up at theb, ahd realize that bany of theb are a huddred tibes larger thad the earth, how does it bake you feel? Yes, we have idvehted the telegraph and the telephode and all the triuphs of our bodern tibes. But whed we look up there, after all we have to recogdize and uhderstad that we are worbs, biserable worbs, ahd dothing else. Ab I right, sir, or ab I wrog? Yes, we are worbs,' he answered himself, and nodded meekly and abjectly in the direction of the firmament.

'Ah, no, he has no literature in his belly,' thought Tonio Kröger. And he recalled something he had lately read, an essay by a famous French writer on cosmological and psychological philosophies, a very delightful *causerie*.

He made some sort of reply to the young man's feeling remarks, and they went on talking, leaning over the rail, and looking into the night with its movement and fitful lights. The young man, it seemed, was a Hamburg merchant on his holiday.

'Y'ought to travel to Copedhagen on the boat, thigks I, and so here I ab, and so far it's been fide. But they shouldn't

have given us the lobster obelet, sir, for it's going to be storby
– the captain said so hibself – and that's do joke with indi-
gestible food like that in your stobach. . . .'

Tonio Kröger listed to all this engaging artlessness and was
privately drawn to it.

'Yes,' he said, 'all the food up here is too heavy. It makes
one lazy and melancholy.'

'Belancholy?' repeated the young man, and looked at him,
taken aback. Then he asked, suddenly: 'You are a stradger
up here, sir?'

'Yes, I come from a long way off,' answered Tonio Kröger
vaguely, waving his arm.

'But you're right,' said the youth; 'Lord kdows you are
right about the belancholy. I am dearly always belancholy, but
specially on evedings like this when there are stars in the sky.'
And he supported his chin again with thumb and forefinger.

'Surely this man writes verses,' thought Tonio Kröger;
'business man's verses, full of deep feeling and single-mindedness.'

Evening drew on. The wind had grown so violent as to
prevent them from talking. So they thought they would sleep
a bit, and wished each other good night.

Tonio Kröger stretched himself out on the narrow cabin
bed, but he found no repose. The strong wind with its sharp
tang had power to rouse him; he was strangely restless with
sweet anticipations. Also he was violently sick with the
motion of the ship as she glided down a steep mountain of
wave and her screw vibrated as in agony, free of the water.
He put on all his clothes again and went up to the deck.

Clouds raced across the moon. The sea danced. It did not
come on in full-bodied, regular waves; but far out in the
pale and flickering light the water was lashed, torn, and
tumbled; leaped upwards like great licking flames; hung in
jagged and fantastic shapes above dizzy abysses, where the
foam seemed to be tossed by the playful strength of colossal

arms and flung upward in all directions. The ship had a heavy passage; she lurched and stamped and groaned through the welter; and far down in her bowels the tiger and the polar bear voiced their acute discomfort. A man in an oilskin, with the hood drawn over his head and a lantern strapped to his chest, went straddling painfully up and down the deck. And at the stern, leaning far out, stood the young man from Hamburg suffering the worst. 'Lord!' he said, in a hollow, quavering voice, when he saw Tonio Kröger. 'Look at the uproar of the elebents, sir!' But he could say no more – he was obliged to turn hastily away.

Tonio Kröger clutched at a taut rope and looked abroad into the arrogance of the elements. His exultation outvied storm and wave; within himself he chanted a song to the sea, instinct with love of her: 'O thou wild friend of my youth. Once more I behold thee – –' But it got no further, he did not finish it. It was not fated to receive a final form or in tranquillity to be welded to a perfect whole. For his heart was too full. . . .

Long he stood; then stretched himself out on a bench by the pilot-house and looked up at the sky, where stars were flickering. He even slept a little. And when the cold foam splashed his face it seemed in his half-dreams like a caress.

Perpendicular chalk-cliffs, ghostly in the moonlight, came in sight. They were nearing the island of Möen. Then sleep came again, broken by salty showers of spray that bit into his face and made it stiff. . . . When he really roused, it was broad day, fresh and palest grey, and the sea had gone down. At breakfast he saw the young man from Hamburg again, who blushed rosy-red for shame of the poetic indiscretions he had been betrayed into by the dark, ruffled up his little red-blond moustache with all five fingers, and called out a brisk and soldierly good morning – after that he studiously avoided him.

And Tonio Kröger landed in Denmark. He arrived in Copenhagen, gave tips to everybody who laid claim to them, took a room at a hotel, and roamed the city for three days with an open guide-book and the air of an intelligent foreigner bent on improving his mind. He looked at the king's New Market and the 'Horse' in the middle of it, gazed respectfully up the columns of the Frauenkirch, stood long before Thorwaldsen's noble and beautiful statuary, climbed the round tower, visited castles, and spent two lively evenings in the Tivoli. But all this was not exactly what he saw.

The doors of the houses – so like those in his native town, with open-work gables of baroque shape – bore names known to him of old; names that had a tender and precious quality, and withal in their syllables an accent of plaintive reproach, of repining after the lost and gone. He walked, he gazed, drawing deep, lingering draughts of moist sea air; and everywhere he saw eyes as blue, hair as blond, faces as familiar, as those that had visited his rueful dreams the night he had spent in his native town. There in the open street it befell him that a glance, a ringing word, a sudden laugh would pierce him to his marrow.

He could not stand the bustling city for long. A restlessness, half memory and half hope, half foolish and half sweet, possessed him; he was moved to drop this rôle of ardently inquiring tourist and lie somewhere, quite quietly, on a beach. So he took ship once more and travelled under a cloudy sky, over a black water, northwards along the coast of Seeland towards Helsingör. Thence he drove, at once, by carriage, for three-quarters of an hour, along and above the sea, reaching at length his ultimate goal, the little white 'bath-hotel' with green blinds. It stood surrounded by a settlement of cottages, and its shingled turret tower looked out on the beach and the Swedish coast. Here he left the carriage, took possession of the light room they had ready for him, filled shelves and presses with his kit, and prepared to stop awhile.

It was well on in September; not many guests were left in

Aalsgaard. Meals were served on the ground floor, in the great beamed dining-room, whose lofty windows led out upon the veranda and the sea. The landlady presided, an elderly spinster with white hair and faded eyes, a faint colour in her cheek and a feeble twittering voice. She was forever arranging her red hands to look well upon the table-cloth. There was a short-necked old gentleman, quite blue in the face, with a grey sailor beard; a fish-dealer he was, from the capital, and strong at the German. He seemed entirely congested and inclined to apoplexy; breathed in short gasps, kept putting his beringed first finger to one nostril, and snorting violently to get a passage of air through the other. Notwithstanding, he addressed himself constantly to the whisky-bottle, which stood at his place at luncheon and dinner, and breakfast as well. Besides him the company consisted only of three tall American youths with their governor or tutor, who kept adjusting his glasses in unbroken silence. All day long he played football with his charges, who had narrow, taciturn faces and reddish-yellow hair parted in the middle. 'Please pass the *wurst*,' said one. 'That's not *wurst*, it's *schinken*,' said the other, and this was the extent of their conversation, as the rest of the time they sat there dumb, drinking hot water.

Tonio Kröger could have wished himself no better table-companions. He revelled in the peace and quiet, listened to the Danish palatals, the clear and the clouded vowels in which the fish-dealer and the landlady desultorily conversed; modestly exchanged views with the fish-dealer on the state of the barometer, and then left the table to go through the veranda and on to the beach once more, where he had already spent long, long morning hours.

Sometimes it was still and summery there. The sea lay idle and smooth, in stripes of blue and russet and bottle-green, played all across with glittering silvery lights. The seaweed shrivelled in the sun and the jelly-fish lay steaming. There was a faintly stagnant smell and a whiff of tar from the fishing-boat against which Tonio Kröger leaned, so standing that he had before his eyes not the Swedish coast but the open horizon and in his face the pure, fresh breath of the softly breathing sea.

Then grey, stormy days would come. The waves lowered their heads like bulls and charged against the beach; they ran and ramped high up the sands and left them strewn with shining wet sea-grass, driftwood and mussels. All abroad beneath an overcast sky extended ranges of billows, and between them foaming valleys palely green; but above the spot where the sun hung behind the cloud a patch like white velvet lay on the sea.

Tonio Kröger stood wrapped in wind and tumult, sunk in the continual dull, drowsy uproar that he loved. When he turned away it seemed suddenly warm and silent all about him. But he was never unconscious of the sea at his back; it called, it lured, it beckoned him. And he smiled.

He went landward, by lonely meadow-paths, and was swallowed up in the beech-groves that clothed the rolling landscape near and far. Here he sat down on the moss against a tree, and gazed at the strip of water he could see between the trunks. Sometimes the sound of surf came on the wind – a noise like boards collapsing at a distance. And from the tree-tops over his head a cawing – hoarse, desolate, forlorn. He held a book on his knee, but did not read a line. He enjoyed profound forgetfulness, hovered disembodied above space and time; only now and again his heart would contract with a fugitive pain, a stab of longing and regret, into whose origin he was too lazy to inquire.

Thus passed some days. He could not have said how many and had no desire to know. But then came one on which something happened; happened while the sun stood in the sky and people were about; and Tonio Kröger, even, felt no vast surprise.

The very opening of the day had been rare and festal.

Tonio Kröger woke early and suddenly from his sleep, with a vague and exquisite alarm; he seemed to be looking at a miracle, a magic illumination. His room had a glass door and balcony facing the sound; a thin white gauze curtain divided it into living- and sleeping-quarters, both hung with delicately tinted paper and furnished with an airy good taste that gave them a sunny and friendly look. But now to his sleep-drunken eyes it lay bathed in a serene and roseate light, an unearthly brightness that gilded walls and furniture and turned the gauze curtain to radiant pink cloud. Tonio Kröger did not at once understand. Not until he stood at the glass door and looked out did he realize that this was the sunrise.

For several days there had been clouds and rain; but now the sky was like a piece of pale-blue silk, spanned shimmering above sea and land, and shot with light from red and golden clouds. The sun's disk rose in splendour from a crisply glittering sea that seemed to quiver and burn beneath it. So began the day. In a joyous daze Tonio Kröger flung on his clothes, and breakfasting in the veranda before everybody else, swam from the little wooden bath-house some distance out into the sound, then walked for an hour along the beach. When he came back, several omnibuses were before the door, and from the dining-room he could see people in the parlour next door where the piano was, in the veranda, and on the terrace in front; quantities of people sitting at little tables enjoying beer and sandwiches amid lively discourse. There were whole families, there were old and young, there were even a few children.

At second breakfast – the table was heavily laden with cold viands, roast, pickled, and smoked – Tonio Kröger inquired what was going on.

'Guests,' said the fish-dealer. 'Tourists and ball-guests from Helsingör. Lord help us, we shall get no sleep this night! There will be dancing and music, and I fear me it will keep up till late. It is a family reunion, a sort of celebration and excursion combined; they all subscribe to it and take advantage of the good weather. They came by boat and bus and they are having breakfast. After that they go on with their drive but at night they will all come back for a dance here in the hall. Yes, damn it, you'll see we shan't get a wink of sleep.'

'Oh, it will be a pleasant change,' said Tonio Kröger.

After that there was nothing more said for some time. The landlady arranged her red fingers on the cloth, the fish-dealer blew through his nostril, the Americans drank hot water and made long faces.

Then all at once a thing came to pass: *Hans Hansen and Ingeborg Holm walked through the room.*

Tonio Kröger, pleasantly fatigued after his swim and rapid walk, was leaning back in his chair and eating smoked salmon on toast; he sat facing the veranda and the ocean. All at once the door opened and the two entered hand-in-hand – calmly and unhurried. Ingeborg, blonde Inge, was dressed just as she used to be at Herr Knaak's dancing-class. The light flowered frock reached down to her ankles and it had a tulle fichu draped with a pointed opening that left her soft throat free. Her hat hung by its ribbons over her arm. She, perhaps, was a little more grown up than she used to be, and her wonderful plait of hair was wound round her head; but Hans Hansen was the same as ever. He wore his sailor overcoat with gilt buttons, and his wide blue sailor collar lay across his shoulders and back; the sailor cap with its short ribbons he was dangling carelessly in his hand. Ingeborg's narrow eyes were turned away; perhaps she felt shy before the company at table. But Hans Hansen turned his head straight towards them and measured one after another defiantly with his steel-blue eyes; challengingly, with a sort of contempt. He even dropped Ingeborg's hand and swung his cap harder than ever, to show what manner of man he was. Thus the two, against the silent, blue-dyed sea, measured the length of the room and passed through the opposite door into the parlour.

This was at half past eleven in the morning. While the guests of the house were still at table the company in the veranda broke up and went away by the side door. No one else came into the dining-room. The guests could hear them laughing and joking as they got into the omnibuses, which rumbled away one by one. . . . 'So they are coming back?' asked Tonio Kröger.

'That they are,' said the fish-dealer. 'More's the pity. They have ordered music, let me tell you – and my room is right above the dining-room.'

'Oh, well, it's a pleasant change,' repeated Tonio Kröger. Then he got up and went away.

That day he spent as he had the others, on the beach and in the wood, holding a book on his knee and blinking in the sun. He had but one thought; they were coming back to have a dance in the hall, the fish-dealer had promised they would, and he did nothing but be glad of this, with a sweet and timorous gladness such as he had not felt through all these long dead years. Once he happened, by some chance association, to think of his friend Adalbert, the novelist, the man who had known what he wanted and betaken himself to the café to get away from the spring. Tonio Kröger shrugged his shoulders at the thought of him.

Luncheon was served earlier than usual, also supper, which they ate in the parlour because the dining-room was being got ready for the ball, and the whole house flung in disorder for the occasion. It grew dark; Tonio Kröger sitting in his room heard on the road and in the house the sounds of approaching festivity. The picnickers were coming back; from Helsingör, by bicycle and carriage, new guests were arriving; a fiddle and a nasal clarinet might be heard practising down in the dining-room. Everything promised a brilliant ball. . . .

Now the little orchestra struck up a march; he could hear the notes, faint but lively. The dancing opened with a polonaise. Tonio Kröger sat for a while and listened. But when he heard the march-time go over into a waltz he got up and slipped noiselessly out of his room.

From his corridor it was possible to go by the side stairs to the side entrance of the hotel and thence to the veranda without passing through a room. He took this route, softly and stealthily as though on forbidden paths, feeling along through the dark, relentlessly drawn by this stupid jigging music, that now came up to him loud and clear.

The veranda was empty and dim, but the glass door stood open into the hall, where shone two large oil lamps, furnished with bright reflectors. Thither he stole on soft feet; and his skin prickled with the thievish pleasure of standing unseen in the dark and spying on the dancers there in the brightly lighted room. Quickly and eagerly he glanced about for the two whom he sought. . . .

Even though the ball was only half an hour old, the merriment seemed in full swing; however, the guests had come hither already warm and merry, after a whole day of carefree, happy companionship. By bending forward a little, Tonio Kröger could see into the parlour from where he was. Several old gentlemen sat there smoking, drinking, and playing cards; others were with their wives on the plush-upholstered chairs in the foreground watching the dance. They sat with their knees apart and their hands resting on them, puffing out their cheeks with a prosperous air; the mothers, with bonnets perched on their parted hair, with their hands folded over their stomachs and their heads on one side, gazed into the whirl of dancers. A platform had been erected on the long side of the hall, and on it the musicians were doing their utmost. There was even a trumpet, that blew with a certain caution, as though afraid of its own voice, and yet after all kept breaking and cracking. Couples were dipping and circling about, others walked arm-in-arm up and down the room. No one wore ballroom clothes; they were dressed as for an outing in the summertime: the men in countrified suits which were obviously their Sunday wear: the girls in light-coloured frocks with bunches of field-flowers in their bodices. Even a few children were there, dancing with each other in their own way, even after the music stopped. There was a long-legged man in a coat with a little swallow-tail, a provincial lion with an eye-glass and frizzed hair, a post-office clerk or some such thing; he was like a comic figure stepped bodily out of a Danish novel; and he seemed to be the leader and manager of the ball. He was everywhere at once, bustling, perspiring, officious, utterly absorbed; setting down his feet in shiny, pointed, military half-boots, in a very artificial and involved manner, toes first; waving his arms to issue an order, clapping his hands for the music to begin; here, there, and everywhere, and glancing over his shoulder in pride at his great bow of office, the streamers of which fluttered grandly in his rear.

Yes, there they were, those two, who had gone by Tonio Kröger in the broad light of day; he saw them again – with a joyful start he recognized them almost at the same moment. Here was Hans Hansen by the door, quite close; his legs apart, a little bent over, he was eating with circumspection a large piece of sponge-cake, holding his hand cupwise under his chin to catch the crumbs. And there by the wall sat Ingeborg Holm, Inge the fair; the post-office clerk was just mincing up to her with an exaggerated bow and asking her to dance. He laid one hand on his back and gracefully shoved the other into his bosom. But she was shaking her head in token that she was a little out of breath and must rest awhile, whereat the post-office clerk sat down by her side.

Tonio Kröger looked at them both, these two for whom he had in the past suffered love – at Hans and Ingeborg. They were Hans and Ingeborg not so much by virtue of individual traits and similarity of costume as by similarity of race and type. This was the blond, fair-haired breed of the steel-blue eyes, which stood to him for the pure, the blithe, the untroubled in life; for a virginal aloofness that was at once both simple and full of pride. . . . He looked at them. Hans Hansen was standing there in his sailor suit, lively and well built as ever, broad in the shoulders and narrow in the hips; Ingeborg was laughing and tossing her head in a certain high-spirited way she had; she carried her hand, a schoolgirl hand, not at all slender, not at all particularly aristocratic, to the back of her head in a certain manner so that the thin sleeve fell away from her elbow – and suddenly such a pang of home-sickness shook his breast that involuntarily he drew farther back into the darkness lest someone might see his features twitch.

'Had I forgotten you?' he asked. 'No, never. Not thee, Hans, not thee, Inge the fair! It was always you I worked for; when I heard applause I always stole a look to see if you were there. . . . Did you read *Don Carlos*, Hans Hansen, as you promised me at the garden gate? No, don't read it! I do not ask it any more. What have you to do with a king who weeps for loneliness? You must not cloud your clear eyes or make them dreamy and dim by peering into melancholy poetry. . . . To be like you! To begin again, to grow up like you, regular like you, simple and normal and cheerful, in conformity and understanding with God and man, beloved of the innocent and happy. To take you, Ingeborg Holm, to wife, and have a son like you, Hans Hansen – to live free from the curse of knowledge and the torment of creation, live and praise God in blessed mediocrity! Begin again? But it would do no good. It would turn out the same – everything would turn out the same as it did before. For some go of necessity astray, because for them there is no such thing as a right path.'

The music ceased; there was a pause in which refreshments were handed round. The post-office assistant tripped about in person with a trayful of herring salad and served the ladies; but before Ingeborg Holm he even went down on one knee as he passed her the dish, and she blushed for pleasure.

But now those within began to be aware of a spectator behind the glass door; some of the flushed and pretty faces turned to measure him with hostile glances; but he stood his ground. Ingeborg and Hans looked at him too, at almost the same time, both with that utter indifference in their eyes that looks so like contempt. And he was conscious, too, of a gaze resting on him from a different quarter; turned his head and met with his own the eyes that had sought him out. A girl stood not far off, with a fine, pale little face – he had already noticed her. She had not danced much, she had few partners, and he had seen her sitting there against the wall, her lip closed in a bitter line. She was standing alone now too; her dress was a thin light stuff, like the others, but beneath the transparent frock her shoulders showed angular and poor, and the thin neck was thrust down so deep between those meagre shoulders that as she stood there motionless she might almost be thought a little deformed. She was holding her hands in their thin mitts across her flat breast, with the finger-tips touching; her head was drooped, yet she was looking up at Tonio Kröger with black swimming eyes. He turned away. . . .

Here, quite close to him, were Ingeborg and Hans. He had sat down beside her – she was perhaps his sister – and they ate and drank together surrounded by other rosy-cheeked folk; they chattered and made merry, called to each other in ringing voices, and laughed aloud. Why could he not go up and speak to them? Make some trivial remark to him or her, to which they might at least answer with a smile? It would make him happy – he longed to do it; he would go back more satisfied to his room if he might feel he had established a little contact with them. He thought out what he might say; but he had not the courage to say it. Yes, this too was just as it had been: they would not understand him, they would listen like strangers to anything he was able to say. For their speech was not his speech.

It seemed the dance was about to begin again. The leader developed a comprehensive activity. He dashed hither and thither, adjuring everybody to get partners; helped the waiters to push chairs and glasses out of the way, gave orders to the musicians, even took some awkward people by the shoulders and shoved them aside. . . . What was coming? They formed squares of four couples each. . . . A frightful memory brought the colour to Tonio Kröger's cheeks. They were forming for a quadrille.

The music struck up, the couples bowed and crossed over. The leader called off; he called off – Heaven save us – in French! And pronounced the nasals with great distinction. Ingeborg Holm danced close by, in the set nearest the glass door. She moved to and fro before him, forwards and back, pacing and turning; he caught a waft from her hair or the thin stuff of her frock and it made him close his eyes with the old, familiar feeling, the fragrance and bitter-sweet enchantment he had faintly felt in all these days, that now filled him utterly with irresistible sweetness. And what was the feeling? Longing, tenderness? Envy? Self-contempt? . . . *Moulinet des dames*. 'Did you laugh, Ingeborg the blonde, did you laugh at me when I disgraced myself by dancing the *moulinet*? And would you still laugh to-day even after I have become something like a famous man? Yes, that you would, and you would be right to laugh. Even if I in my own person had written the nine symphonies and *The World as Will and Idea* and painted the Last Judgement, you would still be eternally right to laugh. . . .' As he looked at her he thought of a line of verse once so familiar to him, now long forgotten: 'I would sleep, but thou must dance.' How well he knew it, that melancholy northern mood it evoked – its heavy inarticulateness. To sleep. . . . To long to be allowed to live the life of simple feeling, to rest sweetly and passively in feeling alone, without compulsion to act and achieve – and yet to be forced to dance, dance the cruel and perilous sword-dance of art;

without even being allowed to forget the melancholy conflict within oneself; to be forced to dance, the while one loved. . . .

A sudden wild extravagance had come over the scene. The sets had broken up, the quadrille was being succeeded by a galop, and all the couples were leaping and gliding about. They flew past Tonio Kröger to a maddeningly quick *tempo*, crossing, advancing, retreating, with quick, breathless laughter. A couple came rushing and circling towards Tonio Kröger; the girl had a pale, refined face and lean, high shoulders. Suddenly, directly in front of him, they tripped and slipped and stumbled. . . . The pale girl fell, so hard and violently it almost looked dangerous; and her partner with her. He must have hurt himself badly, for he quite forgot her, and, half rising, began to rub his knee and grimace; while she, quite dazed, it seemed, still lay on the floor. Then Tonio Kröger came forward, took her gently by the arms, and lifted her up. She looked dazed, bewildered, wretched; then suddenly her delicate face flushed pink.

'*Tak, O, mange tak!*' she said, and gazed up at him with dark, swimming eyes.

'You should not dance any more, Fräulein,' he said gently. Once more he looked round at *them*, at Ingeborg and Hans, and then he went out, left the ball and the veranda and returned to his own room.

He was exhausted with jealousy, worn out with the gaiety in which he had had no part. Just the same, just the same as it had always been. Always with burning cheeks he had stood in his dark corner and suffered for you, you blond, you living, you happy ones! And then quite simply gone away. Somebody *must* come now! Ingeborg *must* notice he had gone, must slip after him, lay a hand on his shoulder and say: 'Come back and be happy. I love you!' But she came not at all. No. such things did not happen. Yes, all was as it had been, and he too was happy, just as he had been. For his heart was alive. But between that past and this present what had happened to make him become that which he now was? Icy desolation, solitude: mind, and art, forsooth!

He undressed, lay down, put out the light. Two names he whispered into his pillow, the few chaste northern syllables that meant for him his true and native way of love, of longing and happiness; that meant to him life and home, meant simple and heartfelt feeling. He looked back on the years that had passed. He thought of the dreamy adventures of the senses, nerves, and mind in which he had been involved; saw himself eaten up with intellect and introspection, ravaged and paralysed by insight, half worn out by the fevers and frosts of creation, helpless and in anguish of conscience between two extremes, flung to and fro between austerity and lust; *raffiné*, impoverished, exhausted by frigid and artificially heightened ecstasies; erring, forsaken, martyred, and ill – and sobbed with nostalgia and remorse.

Here in his room it was still and dark. But from below life's lulling, trivial waltz-rhythm came faintly to his ears.

Tonio Kröger sat up in the north, composing his promised letter to his friend Lisabeta Ivanovna.

'Dear Lisabeta down there in Arcady, whither I shall shortly return,' he wrote: 'here is something like a letter, but it will probably disappoint you, for I mean to keep it rather general. Not that I have nothing to tell; for indeed, in my way, I have had experiences; for instance, in my native town they were even going to arrest me ... but of that by word of mouth. Sometimes now I have days when I would rather state things in general terms than go on telling stories.

'You probably still remember, Lisabeta, that you called me a *bourgeois*, a *bourgeois manqué*? You called me that in an hour when, led on by other confessions I had previously let slip, I confessed to you my love of life, or what

I call life. I ask myself if you were aware how very close
you came to the truth, how much my love of "life" is
one and the same thing as my being a *bourgeois*. This
journey of mine has given me much occasion to ponder
the subject.

'My father, you know, had the temperament of the
north: solid, reflective, puritanically correct, with a
tendency to melancholia. My mother, of indeterminate
foreign blood, was beautiful, sensuous, naïve, passionate
and careless at once, and, I think, irregular by instinct.
The mixture was no doubt extraordinary and bore with
it extraordinary dangers. The issue of it, a *bourgeois* who
strayed off into art, a bohemian who feels nostalgic yearn-
ings for respectability, an artist with a bad conscience.
For surely it is my *bourgeois* conscience makes me see in
the artist life, in all irregularity and all genius, something
profoundly suspect, profoundly disreputable; that fills me
with this lovelorn *faiblesse* for the simple and good, the
comfortably normal, the average unendowed respectable
human being.

'I stand between two worlds. I am at home in neither,
and I suffer in consequence. You artists call me a *bourgeois*,
and the *bourgeois* try to arrest me. . . . I don't know which
makes me feel worse. The *bourgeois* are stupid; but you
adorers of the beautiful, who call me phlegmatic and
without aspirations, you ought to realize that there is a
way of being an artist that goes so deep and is so much a
matter of origins and destinies that no longing seems to
it sweeter and more worth knowing than longing after
the bliss of the commonplace.

'I admire those proud, cold beings who adventure
upon the paths of great and daemonic beauty and despise
"mankind"; but I do not envy them. For if anything is
capable of making a poet of a literary man, it is my *bourgeois* love of the human, the living and usual. It is the

source of all warmth, goodness, and humour; I even almost think it is itself that love of which it stands written that one may speak with the tongues of men and of angels and yet having it not is as sounding brass and tinkling cymbals.

'The work I have so far done is nothing or not much – as good as nothing. I will do better, Lisabeta – this is a promise. As I write, the sea whispers to me and I close my eyes. I am looking into a world unborn and formless, that needs to be ordered and shaped; I see into a whirl of shadows of human figures who beckon to me to weave spells to redeem them: tragic and laughable figures and some that are both together – and to these I am drawn. But my deepest and secretest love belongs to the blond and blue-eyed, the fair and the living, the happy, lovely, and commonplace.

'Do not chide this love, Lisabeta; it is good and fruitful. There is longing in it, and a gentle envy; a touch of contempt and no little innocent bliss.'

1903

THOMAS MANN

CONFESSIONS OF FELIX KRULL

'Here is that unheard of, that supposedly impossible thing, a good German comic novel – a marvellously good one. There was nothing about Mann's other later novels to suggest that anything like *Felix Krull* was in store; and nothing else in modern German literature has prepared the way for it' – Edwin Muir in the *Listener*.

DOCTOR FAUSTUS

Doctor Faustus, the life of the German composer, Adrian Leverkühn is one of the most convincing accounts of genius ever written. Thomas Mann charts Leverkühn's extraordinary career from his precocious childhood to his tragic death – when Leverkühn reveals the horrifying price he had to pay for his achievement.

THE HOLY SINNER

An epic of arch-sinfulness – witting and unwitting – based on the life of Grigorss, natural child of the Duke of Flanders by his sister, who after various adventures inadvertently married his own mother, but after many years of solitary penance was proclaimed Pope in Rome.

LOTTE IN WEIMAR

Forty-four years after their youthful association, Lotte Kestner, real-life heroine of Goethe's famous novel *The Sorrows of Young Werther*, makes a pilgrimage to Weimar to see Goethe. Mann gives a masterly portrayal of a creative genius, polymath and politician, and his influence on his contemporaries.

THE MAGIC MOUNTAIN

A cosmopolitan collection of people are confined in a sanatorium high in the Swiss Alps. In spite of their isolation, love, war, and emotions all affect and influence their conversation and they stand as a microcosm of the sick European society which lies below them. *The Magic Mountain* won the Nobel Prize for Literature in 1929.

also available

BUDDENBROOKS
LITTLE HERR FRIEDEMANN AND OTHER STORIES
MARIO AND THE MAGICIAN AND OTHER STORIES

Not for sale in the U.S.A. or Canada